VEGETARIAN

Pack Law 5

Becca Van

MENAGE EVERLASTING

Siren Publishing, Inc.
www.SirenPublishing.com

A SIREN PUBLISHING BOOK
IMPRINT: Ménage Everlasting

VEGETARIAN MATE
Copyright © 2012 by Becca Van

ISBN: 978-1-62242-046-9

First Printing: November 2012

Cover design by Les Byerley
All art and logo copyright © 2012 by Siren Publishing, Inc.

Printed in the U.S.A.

PUBLISHER
Siren Publishing, Inc.
www.SirenPublishing.com

DEDICATION

This book is dedicated to Rochelle Martin of the UK, for her suggestion of a coming-soon tag for my website and for advising ways to make it happen. My heroine is named after you, Rochelle! Thank you!

VEGETARIAN MATE

Pack Law 5

BECCA VAN
Copyright © 2012

Chapter One

Rochelle Murphy was lost. Seriously lost. She'd meant to pull over hours ago and find a place to stay for the night, but she hadn't seen anything bigger than a gas station in the past hour. Even finding one of those would be welcome, since she didn't think she could hold her bladder for much longer.

She settled for pulling over on the shoulder. She wrenched the GPS off the dash and smacked the side of it with her hand. The thing had gone on the fritz over two hours ago, and even though she had been on the lookout for road signs, she hadn't seen anything that would direct her back to the interstate. In fact, she hadn't really been paying attention. She so loved listening to the radio and singing along that she got caught up in it and little else registered in her brain.

Chagrinned by that thought, she turned down the radio. It was time to concentrate. If she didn't find a bathroom soon, she might just have to pull off the side of the road and go behind a tree. Rochelle shuddered at the thought. She was a woman who liked her modern conveniences.

Rochelle squinted into the darkness, but there was nothing ahead. Sighing, she pulled back onto the road.

The silence of the car weighed on her, but she didn't turn the radio back up. *I'm just tired.* She'd been on the road for a month after leaving her dead-end job, leasing out the room of the apartment she had shared with another girl, and taking off. She wanted to see some of her own country and then maybe, when she could afford it, some of the world. Her hometown of Evansville, Kentucky, just hadn't felt right to her, and she had no family to tie her there. So she had set out on an adventure to find what she felt in her heart was waiting for her.

Haven't found it yet, either.

She told herself to cut it out. She liked this carefree life. She'd worked her way across three states, stopping wherever she wanted and getting employment in diners, pubs, or supermarkets to replenish her cash supply. It had given her a freedom that she thought she'd never be able to sacrifice, but Rochelle still wasn't happy. Not that she was sad. She just felt that something was missing from her life.

But she wasn't going to wait for whatever that was to come to her. Rochelle intended to find what she was looking for by herself.

She squirmed in her seat. The only thing she needed to find right this second, though, was a bathroom. Her situation was getting downright painful.

She nearly gasped out loud when she saw lights in the distance. The lights flashed through the trees intermittently, and by the time she spied a large wrought-iron gate to what had to be a private property, she was wiggling in her seat and her bladder felt like it was about to burst.

The last thing she wanted to do was go behind a tree, so she did the only thing she could think of. Rochelle pulled into the entry of the drive and eyed the small box off the side of the gate. Beyond desperation, she got out of her car and pushed the button. As she did, she saw golden eyes glowing in the darkness just off the drive on the other side of the gates. She jumped about a foot off the ground when what appeared to be a large wolf moved toward her, sniffing the air.

Just as she was about to run back and dive into her car, a deep voice came over the intercom.

"Yes, can I help you?"

With her eyes still pinned on the wolf, Rochelle cleared her throat and tried to speak. The first thing that popped out of her mouth wasn't what she had intended to say.

"There's a wolf."

"Yes, don't worry about it. The wolf won't hurt you. What can I do for you?"

Shivers raced up and down her spine as the deep cadence of the disembodied voice washed over her, causing goose bumps to erupt all over her body.

"Uh, I know I'm being a little forward and probably rude. But I've been traveling for hours and am lost. I would really appreciate it if I could use your restroom."

Rochelle cursed the breathy desperation she heard in her own voice and placed her hand over her aching bladder as she danced from one foot to the other, waiting with bated breath for an answer.

"Sure. Come up the drive to the house, and I'll meet you out front."

A click sounded, and Rochelle presumed the man had disconnected the intercom. The gates began to open silently. She ran back to her car, hoping the wolf wouldn't get to her before she made it, and sighed with relief when she had the door closed. Searching as best she could through the dark, she couldn't spot the wolf. Her overfull bladder caused her to moan in pain, but she put her car into *drive* and headed up the driveway.

When the house finally came into view, she gasped in awe. It was huge. She didn't think houses were built like this one anymore and felt a little overwhelmed that she had obviously stopped at some rich asshole's mansion.

Her imagination brought forth an eccentric elderly man with gray hair and a body made beefy from too much easy living. The owner would have to be eccentric to let a wolf roam the grounds. But she couldn't have been more wrong.

She stared as she slowed her car near the entry and gaped as the biggest, most muscular mountain of a man she'd ever seen came down the steps. His bald head gleamed under the lights and his shoulders rippled beneath the knit cotton of his T-shirt. Standing at around six foot five and probably coming in at two hundred and eighty pounds, he looked like a linebacker with his massive biceps and pecs and his strong, brawny thighs. A jagged scar ran from just above his left eyebrow and down his cheek, but instead of detracting from his looks, it immediately brought to mind swashbuckling pirates. But the mark reminded her of the wolf she had seen and the claws it no doubt had.

Rochelle opened her door before he reached it and stood. She didn't want to feel even more intimidated by meeting the man sitting on her ass.

"Hi, I'm Jarrod Friess. And you are?"

"Rochelle Murphy. I'm sorry for disturbing your evening, but thank you from the bottom of my heart," she said with another little wiggle.

"If you would like to come inside, I'll let you use the bathroom." She saw his mouth twitch with amusement, but that wasn't the only emotion on his face. The heated look in his eyes gave her pause. But she was too distressed to worry about him just then.

"Thanks," Rochelle squeaked, slamming her car door closed and following Jarrod inside.

"Take the set of stairs up the first landing and turn left, follow the hall down to the end, and take a right. The bathroom is the fourth door down on the left," he stated. Rochelle did her best to listen from the semitrance she was in, drowning in the blue depths of his eyes. The spell only broke when he closed those eyes and inhaled as if he was sniffing her. Rochelle frowned, but she was too desperate to question what he was doing.

Rochelle literally ran up the stairs and took a left. After that she took a right but forgot which door he said led to the bathroom. She cautiously opened each door and was thankful when she didn't encounter anyone. By the third door, she was so close to peeing herself she didn't think she could walk another step. She walked into the opulent bathroom, closing and locking the door behind her, and scanned the interior. *Shit. Shit. Shit. No toilet. I can't wait.*

Decision made, Rochelle unsnapped her jeans and pulled her pants down. She lifted her ass over the edge of the sink, used her hands to grip the sides, and scooted back a little. Her feet left the floor, and she ended up with the cold sink digging into her legs at midthigh from beneath and sighed with relief. The sink would have to do. Just as she was about to get down from her precarious perch, a vibration made her clutch the rim tighter. She hit the floor with a squeak, and pain exploded in her head. That was the last thing she remembered as she slipped into unconsciousness.

* * * *

Malcolm Friess had gone for a run before dinner to relieve the stress after a long day at work. He and his brothers, Jarrod and Braxton, all worked at the Aztec Sheriff's Department. Earlier that day they had attended a traffic accident and, much to their horror, children had been injured. The kids would survive, thank God, but he hated knowing about or seeing any form of injury to a child. After changing forms, he had lit out around the grounds of the den house, trying to relieve the ache and tightness in his muscles. Just as he neared the entry gate, he heard a car slow and saw headlights gleaming through the wrought-iron gate.

Malcolm wound his way along the fence line and stayed out of sight while sniffing the air. The tension which had only just left came back in full force, but this time for an entirely different reason. He stepped into the clearing and stared intently at the delectable woman on the other side of the gate. She was so close and yet so far away. Her delicious scent wafted toward him on the breeze, hardening every muscle in his body. His cock filled with blood, and he kept to the shadows as he crept closer to the gate. The sound of a car door being opened caused his ears to twitch forward. He stood still as her light-blue eyes pinned him with nervous intensity and then heard the intercom buzzer being pushed.

Jarrod answered the call, and since he wanted to get closer to the woman on the other side of the fence, he spoke to his older brother, using their private mind link.

"Mate!" He pushed the word to his brothers and stepped onto the side of the gravel drive. Her eyes connected with his, making her jump, and he knew without a doubt he was going to do everything within his power to keep this woman at the pack house.

Malcolm listened to her talk to Jarrod and watched her return to her car. He backed up and merged with the shadows once more, not wanting to frighten her in his animal form. Keeping pace with her car, he ran alongside the drive, knowing she wasn't even aware of his presence. Staying at the edge of the trees, he watched as Jarrod greeted Rochelle Murphy and led her into the den.

Malcolm ran around the side of the house and changed back to his human form. Brax was waiting at the side door with his clothes. After quickly dressing, he rushed inside, joining his brothers as they stood at the bottom of the stairs. Inhaling deeply, he groaned as his cock pulsed and his balls ached. The scent of raspberries assailed his nostrils, ratcheting up his desire even more. Just as he was about to ask his brother if he had talked to her as he led her inside, a rumble sounded, and then a loud crash and a thud reverberated against his eardrum.

Malcolm and his brothers sprinted up the stairs and down the hall. Jarrod burst into the bathroom, the lock giving away beneath his weight, with Malcolm and Brax right behind. His mate was out cold on the floor with her jeans and panties down around her ankles. The sink which had been on the wall in the bathroom was broken in pieces behind her. He felt like laughing and also felt deep concern for his unconscious woman.

Obviously she hadn't been able to find the toilet and had used the facilities on hand. "Shit," Jarrod growled, but his lips twitched and his eyes twinkled with amusement. "Help me get her covered up and call Blayk. We need him to check her over."

Malcolm reached out for her panties and moaned as his hand connected with the silky-smooth skin of her calf. He let his eyes wander over her as he and Brax pulled her undies up. Her hair was a combination of gold and darker blonde and long enough to reach the top of her ass. Her eyebrows were light golden, and her lashes, which formed crescents against her pale cheeks, were a contrasting ebony. She was average height with full hips and shapely thighs, which he could just imagine wrapped around his hips.

He inhaled her sweet fragrance once more, and his eyes alighted on the light sprinkling of freckles across the bridge of her nose. Her lips were a pale pink, and he wanted to lean down and taste her but restrained himself. Malcolm didn't want to take advantage of her and was growing even more concerned that she didn't show any signs of coming around.

Jarrod carefully lifted her hips so that he and Brax could pull her jeans up and fasten them. When she was once more decent, his brother picked her up and carried her out of the bathroom, along the corridor, and back down the stairs. He followed in Jarrod's wake to the back of the house, where Blayk's office was set up.

One of the others must have signaled the doctor, since Blayk was waiting for them. Jarrod carefully placed her on the exam table.

"What the hell happened?"

"Uh, she had an accident," Jarrod replied in a strangled voice.

"Well, I figured." Blayk frowned at Jarrod. "Can you be more specific? I want to know how you found her."

"I think she hit her head on the floor in the bathroom," Malcolm stated through a tight throat.

"How the hell did she end up on the floor?" Blayk muttered as he examined their mate.

Malcolm couldn't answer. He was torn between concern and hilarity and was having a hard time controlling his mirth.

"She has a good-size knot on the side of her head, just above her right ear. Other than that she appears to be fine." Blayk lifted her eyelids and flashed light onto her pupils to check their response. "She has a slight concussion. She'll need to keep quiet for a couple of days. Who is she?"

"Mate," Brax snarled at Blayk, who quickly withdrew his hands from her and stepped back.

Rochelle moaned and drew in a deep breath. Reaching up, she winced when her fingers connected with the lump on her head.

"Shit a brick. What the…"

"Are you all right, Rochelle?" Jarrod asked, concern evident in his voice.

Rochelle's eyes popped open, and she slowly looked from Jarrod to Braxton, himself, and Blayk.

"What happen…" she began to ask and then must have remembered. Her cheeks turned first pink and then a bright-red hue. Covering her face with her hands, her shoulders shook.

Her voice came out muffled. "God sakes."

Malcolm bit his lip when he heard a gurgling noise come from Jarrod. He smiled at the quirk she had put to the familiar phrase "for God's sake." Obviously their mate wasn't a woman bound by conformity. He looked up at his brother and saw he was barely containing his humor. Brax shifted at his side, drawing his gaze. His brother had a smile as wide as Texas on his face. That was all it took.

Malcolm burst out laughing, and once he started he couldn't stop. He fell to his knees clutching his stomach and hoped his mate understood he wasn't laughing because she was injured. Tears rolled down his face, and he glanced at his brothers through misty eyes as their raucous laughter joined his. Blayk was standing off to the side of the exam bed looking totally perplexed, and that only made him laugh harder. Malcolm couldn't even stop when his mate sat up on the bed, glaring at them.

Blayk reached out to steady her when she stood and swayed. That wiped the amusement from him in an instant. His hilarity turned to deep growls until Blayk just glared at him and helped Rochelle to sit on the side of the bed before she fell down.

For some reason his growling made his mate's mouth twitch and she went from glaring daggers at him and his brothers to amusement and then full-blown joviality. But her humor didn't last long. She groaned and then clutched her head in obvious pain.

"God, how embarrassing," she whispered. "I'll pay for the damage."

"Shh, it's okay, baby. We'll cover it," Jarrod told her with a smile.

"No. I will pay for the damage. I need to get moving."

"No. You can't drive with a concussion, ma'am. I wouldn't want you on the road with a head injury. You'll be a danger to others as well as yourself."

"Who are you?"

"I'm Dr. Blayk Friess."

"Oh, well then at least you know what you're talking about," Rochelle muttered and closed her eyes.

"Thanks. I think."

Jarrod snorted and moved in close to Rochelle. She looked up quickly and winced at the movement. "Rochelle, these are my brothers, Malcolm and Braxton. Since you aren't allowed to drive, why don't I take you up to our spare room and you can get settled in for the night?"

"Who found me?"

"My brothers and I did," Malcolm answered, moving forward. He held out a hand in greeting and nearly went to his knees with a groan when her skin met his. His wolf pushed at him, wanting him to claim his mate, but he got the upper hand and pushed his animal back down.

"Shit," Rochelle whispered, pulling her hand away from his and slipping off the table, only to sway once more. "I can't stay here. I have to leave. Just let me get my checkbook from my car and I'll cover the cost of the damage."

"You aren't driving anywhere, young lady. You had better let these three settle you into their spare room and lie down before you fall down," Blayk said sternly.

"Who are you bossing around?"

Talia, Blayk's mate, stood in the doorway with her hands on her hips and her chin lifted. Malcolm held in a grin as she ignored Blayk's eye roll and shoved her way in between him and Jarrod.

"I'm Talia Friess," she said, offering her hand. "The bossy guy over there is my husband."

Malcolm watched as Rochelle hesitantly reached out and shook hands, introducing herself.

"Are you okay?"

"Yeah, thanks."

"I'll bet you're hungry and thirsty. Why don't you come on out to the dining room and we'll get you something to eat?"

Malcolm heard Rochelle's stomach grumble, and she sighed as if with resignation.

"Thank you so much. I don't want to put any of you out."

"You're not," Talia replied with a smile. "Come on. You can lean on me. Your head must be killing you."

Malcolm and his brothers followed Talia and their mate out of Blayk's office, down the hall, and into the large dining room. All the way there, he cursed himself for not suggesting that Rochelle lean on his shoulder instead.

Chapter Two

Rochelle leaned against Talia as she was led into a large dining room which was connected to a massive gourmet kitchen. Even though her head felt like a bass drum had taken up residence where her brain was supposed to be, she was actually quite hungry. Cringing internally as each step she took made the throb behind her skull worse, she felt her cheeks heat again as she thought over how Jarrod and his brothers would have found her.

She was such a klutz. She was embarrassed to think the three Friess brothers must have found her on the floor with her jeans and panties around her ankles. Her full bladder might have been uncomfortable, but now she was in even more pain and feeling very humiliated as well.

She must have looked one hell of a sight when they found her. She didn't blame them for busting a gut laughing, but why did it have to be such incredibly handsome men who found her? Jarrod with his tall, muscular body, bald head, and that roguish scar was matched in good looks by both his brothers. Malcolm had collar-length brown hair, green eyes, wide shoulders, and long legs, which kept drawing her eyes. Braxton's eyes were more green than blue and his hair was a sandy color. He wasn't as brawny as Jarrod, but none of the men were lacking in the muscle department.

The Friess brothers were so similar in looks they might have been triplets, except that Malcolm looked to be a couple of years younger than Jarrod, and maybe a year or two separated Jarrod from Braxton. Malcolm was an inch shorter than Jarrod and Braxton was an inch taller. Who knew she would meet such gigantic, sexy men when she had left her hometown? Not that she was complaining. She liked eye candy as much as the next woman.

You're staring, girl. Get a grip!

Talia's voice drew her from her speculation. "Come and meet my other husbands."

What? Husbands? She has more than one?

Talia led her over to the humungous table and introduced her to Chris and James Friess, her *other* husbands. She had already indicated that Blayk was her husband when she had come into the clinic.

She has three husbands? How the hell is that even possible? And who the hell wants to put up with more than one male?

"Nice to meet you," Rochelle muttered and hoped her perplexity didn't show. Then Talia led her over to the head of the table, where three men crowded around another woman.

"Rochelle, these are the Al—heads of the family, Jonah, Mikhail, and Brock Friess, and their wife, Michelle."

"Pleased to meet you," Rochelle responded again. *Another woman with three husbands? Have I fallen into the Twilight Zone? What the fuck?* This went on another two times, and Rochelle wondered if she should get the hell out of Dodge. The room was packed full of males and only a handful of females. Did all the men in this house share their women? She was definitely going to eat and run.

Jarrod had trailed her and Talia around the room. "Come on, baby. Let's get you seated so you can eat and lie down. You look as if you are about to pass out." Jarrod took her hand and led her to the other end of the table, where Malcolm and Braxton were seated.

He pulled a chair out for her and then sat beside her. The food was brought in by the housekeeper, Angie, and her daughter, Cindy, whom Malcolm introduced her to, and then he reached for her plate and began loading it with food. By the time he was done, the plate was piled high with meat and very few vegetables. It would have fed her for a week if she'd been willing to eat it at all. Her stomach roiled just looking at it.

He really doesn't think I'm going to eat all that, does he?

When he placed the heaped plate in front of her, she stared at it in horror. She knew she wasn't wafer thin, but geez, she wasn't fat either.

When Malcolm picked up his empty plate, she snatched it from his hand, picked up the one in front of her with her free hand, her wrist wobbling under the weight, and quickly put it in front of him. He looked at her with a raised brow and a smirk but didn't say anything, so she turned away, ignoring him.

Rochelle's stomach rebelled at the smell of meat. There was no way she was touching anything on the table that had ever had a heartbeat, and she quietly set about placing vegetables on her plate. She began to eat and slowly became aware of the silence which had descended on the room. Looking up, she found every eye on her. Shifting in her seat, she lowered her eyes, hoping they didn't see how embarrassed she was. When the silence became too much, she looked up and turned her glare to Jarrod, Braxton, and Malcolm.

"What?" she snarled.

"You're not eating any meat." Braxton stated the obvious.

"Well, duh. I'm a vegetarian," she said, glaring at him as if daring him to make something out of it.

Several chuckles, guffaws, and snorts sounded around the table. Rochelle felt her cheeks burn even hotter and lowered her head. Then she decided she didn't care what they thought and looked up again.

"Do you have a problem with that?" she snapped and looked at the men beside her then on to each man who dared to smile or laugh.

"No, baby, we don't care what you eat," Jarrod said with a quirk of his lips. "Neither does anyone else."

Rochelle caught him glaring at a few of the younger males, and they immediately bowed their heads as if in genuflection. *What the hell is wrong with these people? First they share a wife, and now some of them lower their heads as if in submission. Well, it looks like you took a wrong turn at Albuquerque and ended up on Marvin the Martian's home planet.*

But even as she thought that, her body was tingling at the close proximity of Jarrod, Braxton, and Malcolm. Every time Jarrod moved, his arm brushed against hers, sending warm, tingly pulses through her body. *Why the hell does my body have to go haywire now? Why couldn't it have waited another month or another thousand or so miles?*

Shifting in her seat to relieve the pressure of her jeans on her aching clit, she heard Malcolm inhale at her other side and turned to watch him surreptitiously from beneath her eyelashes. He leaned in toward her slightly and sniffed, his eyes closing as if he smelled a freshly baked apple pie. A groan from Jarrod's other side drew her attention, and she looked up to see Braxton smelling the air and looking at her as if he was about to devour her. *Can they smell my arousal? No, that's not possible!*

Is it?

"Eat up, baby, then we'll take you upstairs so you can lie down," Jarrod said in a deep, rumbling voice, causing her skin to once more erupt in gooseflesh.

"My name is Rochelle!"

Rochelle placed her silverware on her plate. She was done. Her head was throbbing like a bitch, and so was her pussy. She had to get away from them, and she was in too much pain to even contemplate driving anywhere, and she was also starting to feel a little queasy. No doubt because of the pounding in her head and the smell of meat.

"Take her upstairs, now," Blayk commanded from further down the table.

Rochelle didn't protest when Jarrod pulled back her chair and helped her to her feet. Nor when he lifted her into his arms and strode out of the room. She closed her eyes and let the drowsiness take over, the slight rocking of Jarrod's movement nearly putting her to sleep. Rousing slightly when she was placed onto a bed, she didn't protest when gentle hands removed her shoes, jeans, and sweater. Rolling to her side, she burrowed into the pillow and let sleep claim her.

* * * *

Jarrod couldn't believe that the beautiful, sassy woman with golden-blonde hair and brilliant blue eyes was their mate. The minute she had opened her car door, he knew Malcolm had been right. Her scent called to his wolf, and he had been battling with his inner beast ever since. His animal wanted to claim its mate, but he controlled it by ignoring the urge to bite.

Sitting on the side of the bed in the guest room of the suite he shared with his brothers, he stared down at her. She looked so pale and fragile, but he knew that was a misconception. From what he had seen so far, their little mate was a feisty little thing and also resourceful. He smiled again and thought about how he was going to explain the damage to the upstairs bathroom to his Alphas and cousins, Jonah, Mikhail, and Brock. He decided honesty was the best policy and hoped they would see the humor in the situation like he and his brothers had.

Jarrod knew damn well every *were* in the house had heard that crash upstairs and was curious about it, but since he told everyone through the common pack link he and his brothers were investigating, they hadn't worried too much. He didn't have a problem covering the cost of the damage his mate had done to the sink, but he wasn't so sure she was going to be as acquiescent.

She'd already proven she had backbone when she had shoved the plate Malcolm had filled for her at him and then when she had challenged the snickers over her vegetarianism.

He was just thankful she hadn't glared at his Alphas when she had taken a stand. Unconsciously challenging the leaders of the Friess pack could have ended in trouble. Jarrod just hoped that Rochelle stuck around and after they told her what they were wouldn't run from them thinking they were crazy. He brushed the hair back from her pale face, inhaling her delectable fruity scent, closing his eyes as his cock throbbed against the zipper of his jeans. They had waited so long for their mate, and he couldn't wait to start the courting process.

"She is so fucking sexy," Malcolm whispered from the doorway. He had moved back across the room after helping him make their mate comfortable to sleep. Jarrod knew he was keeping his distance on purpose and wondered why he was torturing himself by remaining so close to her. Braxton was leaning against the wall next to the door.

"Yes, she is."

"She is probably going to want to leave in the morning," Braxton said with a sigh. "How the hell are we going to get her to stay?"

"I don't know," replied Jarrod. "But one thing is certain. We are going to have to do our best at talking her into staying."

"Hopefully she'll feel better after a good night's rest," Malcolm suggested. "She may be more inclined to listen once she's feeling well."

"God, I hope so." Jarrod rose to his feet as his brothers exited the room. Giving one last look over his shoulder at the woman who had already changed their lives but didn't even know it, he slowly pulled the door closed. He was downstairs in his Alphas' office moments later, explaining the reason for the damage to the upstairs bathroom.

After the laughter had died down, Jarrod handed over a check which would cover the cost of repairs. He didn't mind doing his part to take care of his mate.

He just hoped she didn't balk when they tried to keep her around.

Chapter Three

Rochelle woke up feeling a little stiff and sore. She groaned as she stretched, stunned by her bad luck. *Why is it that whenever I get an epiphany, deciding to find myself, things always goes awry? God sakes, girl, you are just a clumsy klutz. It's a wonder I've lived long enough to reach twenty-four.*

Thinking back over her past injuries and her latest embarrassing incident made her cringe. *What must those three sexy-looking men think of me?* God, she didn't think she could face them again without her cheeks turning red.

Well, there's no use crying over spilt milk, girl. Get up, get dressed, and leave. Yeah, now there's a plan.

Feeling a little better after making a decision, she swung her feet over the side of the bed and groaned as her still-sore head made its presence known. The pain wasn't as bad as last night, but she was going to have to move a little more slowly and cautiously than usual. *Oh, that should help with my klutz tendencies!*

Rochelle had figured out a couple of years back that she often walked into furniture, walls, and just about anything else because she was always in such a hurry. Even when she tried to slow down, objects seemed to jump out into her path.

Chuckling at her vivid imagination, she peeked into the open door off the side of the room.

"Oh. My. God."

The en suite bathroom was nearly big enough to have a party in. On the far wall was a spa large enough to seat six people. Two sinks were set into the counter with gleaming, elegant, long-necked taps.

The shower was a large glassed-in cubicle with shower sprays at intermittent intervals but enough so that at least three people could bathe at once and not miss out on any of the water. To the right she saw another door, which turned out to conceal the toilet.

Why the hell would they need a bathroom this size? Think about it, girl. How many husbands did those women have? Oh yeah. That explains it.

After showering and dressing, Rochelle repacked the bag someone had thoughtfully brought up from her car. Slinging her purse over her shoulder, she glanced about, looking for anything she may have left behind as she moved toward the door. Just as she turned back, her shoulder connected with the wooden doorjamb with a loud crack. "Ow!" Dropping her bag and purse, she clutched at her shoulder and went down to her knees. "God sakes, you are such a klutz!"

"Are you all right, baby?"

"Shit, just what I need. Another witness to my clumsiness," she muttered under her breath. Removing her hands from her body, she slowly looked up. Starting at the black boots, her gaze travelled up denim-encased shins, bulging, muscular thighs, over a hard, flat stomach and pectorals covered in black cotton, and ended up at Jarrod's startling blue eyes.

He reached down, wrapped his massive hands around her upper arms, and lifted her from the floor with ease. Her feet dangled for a moment or two, and she only released a breath when they were once again touching the floor. But he didn't let her go. She tried to pull back, but his firm grip prevented her.

"Easy, baby, I just want to make sure you're steady on your feet."

"I'm fine," Rochelle snapped and then realized how ungrateful she must sound. She always became a little snarky when others saw how clumsy she was, because of embarrassment. "Sorry. Thank you, but I'm okay."

Taking a step back when he finally let her go, she exhaled in relief. *God sakes, he is hot.* She couldn't seem to tear her eyes away from him.

"Where were you going, Rochelle?"

"Uh, I was taking my stuff down to my car."

"You haven't even had breakfast yet, baby. I can help you with your things later. Come on downstairs and eat." Jarrod held out a hand to her.

Taking a deep breath, she placed her hand in his and exhaled as their skin touched. It didn't make one bit of difference. Those tingling pulses still raced up her arm and over her breasts, causing her areolas to prickle and her nipples to harden. Then the warmth spread down her torso into her belly to pool in her pussy. *Oh God. One touch and I'm horny! What the hell?*

Rochelle let Jarrod lead her from the suite and down the stairs. Her stomach rumbled as the scent of food reached her. The dining room was just as full as it had been the night before, but this time the people didn't take much notice of her. *Thank you, God!*

Jarrod saw her seated next to Malcolm and then sat beside her. She eyed the food platters, which again contained mostly steak and bacon. Her stomach rumbled again, but this time in protest. No matter how often she tried to eat meat, Rochelle just couldn't get past the fact that it had once been a living, feeling creature. A mug of coffee was placed in front of her, and she looked up to smile her thanks at Cindy. The young woman was looking at Jarrod, Malcolm, and Braxton nervously, but when she caught Rochelle watching, she smiled.

"Would you like some toast or cereal for breakfast?" She practically whispered her question.

"Toast would be nice. Thank you."

Once Rochelle was finished with breakfast, she picked up her mug of coffee and surreptitiously studied the occupants of the room. The men were all so big and handsome, but none of them drew her like

Jarrod, Malcolm, and Braxton. Maybe the men here were so big because they all seemed to eat so much meat. She shuddered and looked down at her plate.

"Rochelle, I think you should stay here at least another night," Jarrod said and held up his hand when she would have spoken. "Let me finish. Blayk has already suggested you shouldn't drive for a couple of days. Victims of concussion tend to get sleepy, and I couldn't live with my conscience if you drove off and then had an accident. Please consider delaying your departure for another few days."

Rochelle felt warm and fuzzy inside over his concern for her, and since she still had a headache and was feeling a little tired she decided he was right.

"Okay. Thank you for the offer of your hospitality. I'll try and keep out of everyone's way."

"That's not necessary, Rochelle." Jarrod rose to his feet. "Treat this place like you would your own home. We'll feel a lot better knowing you are safe and healing without causing any accidents or putting yourself in danger. Now, we have to get ready for work. We'll see you later."

Jarrod and his brothers headed for their rooms, so she took the opportunity to approach the "bosses."

Rising from her seat, she walked toward Michelle and her husbands.

"Hi, Rochelle, have a seat." Michelle shoved at her husband Mikhail's shoulder until he got up and moved to another chair.

"Hi," she began as she tried to figure out what she was going to say. "Um, I–I had a bit of an accident in the bathroom upstairs last night and would like to pay for the damage."

She thought she saw Michelle's lips twitch, but when she looked again she realized she must have imagined it. *She can't possibly know. Can she?* She looked up and saw the gleam of amusement in Michelle's eyes. *Oh shit! Does everyone know what happened?*

"You don't need to worry. Jarrod's already taken care of it."

Rochelle slid her eyes to the two men on the other side of Michelle and caught them smiling. They looked away quickly when they saw her looking at them. *Oh, how fucking embarrassing!*

"They told you!"

"They didn't want to, honey, but Jarrod had to explain why he was handing a check over to Jonah."

"Oh shit. I can't believe they…I'm sorry. I have to go." There was no way she could stay now. "Thanks for your hospitality," she whispered and pushed her chair back quickly.

She was in such a hurry to leave her feet got caught in the legs of her chair. Hands reached out to steady her, and she turned her head to thank them again without slowing down. She didn't see the cart Angie had just wheeled up to the table until it was too late. She was moving so fast that momentum carried her forward.

Up and over she went. The glass on top of the cart cracked under her when she reached out, and as she toppled over, it flipped and landed on top of her. The weakened glass shattered. Rochelle threw up her arms to protect her face. A large shard of glass sliced into the underside of her forearm, going deep. White-hot burning pain seared into her soft skin, and she cried out.

Somewhere behind her, someone roared, "Fuck." In moments, she was surrounded by large male bodies.

"Don't touch her," Blayk yelled from across the room. If she hadn't seen it with her own eyes, she wouldn't have believed how fast he moved. One moment he was across the room, and the next he was at her side.

"Shit, baby. You're a hazard to yourself," Jarrod muttered.

Looking up at him she saw he was dressed in a sheriff's uniform. His brothers Braxton and Malcolm were behind him, and they had on deputy uniforms. They looked so damn hot in their uniforms, and if she hadn't been in pain, she may have drooled at the sight of them.

"We need to get her into my office. From the amount of blood pouring out, I think she's nicked an artery," Blayk stated calmly. "That glass has to stay in her arm until I can take a closer look. It could be all that's stopping her from bleeding out. Don't jostle her too much when you lift her."

Rochelle whimpered as Jarrod carefully picked her up, but it wasn't from pain. She hated the sight of blood, especially when it was her own. Closing her eyes, she gulped in air as she began to feel light-headed. When she opened them again, she was once more back on the exam table in Blayk's infirmary. She wondered if she had passed out for a moment or two.

Blayk pulled over a large lamp with a magnifying glass attached. After inspecting the wound, which still had the large shard of glass protruding from it, he walked over to a cupboard, rummaged around, and came back with a tray full of silver sterilized tools as well as two hypodermic needles.

"I'm going to give you a local anesthetic so I can work without causing you pain. Okay?"

After swallowing loudly, Rochelle still couldn't seem to find her voice, so she gave a nod. She hissed through her teeth as the sharp needle pierced her skin but kept still. She was such a wuss when it came to anything medical. Just the thought of going to the doctor could nearly make her swoon.

Turning her head away from the blood, she looked up to see Jarrod, Malcolm, and Braxton watching her with concern. Her face flamed red hot, and she knew it had probably changed color as well. She turned to look back at Blayk when he began to speak.

"Talia, honey, can you come and give me a hand?" Blayk hadn't looked away from her arm.

Talia? Talia's not here. As Rochelle was beginning to wonder how hard she'd banged her head last night, she heard the door open. Talia appeared at her side a moment later, saying, "Sure. What do you want me to do?"

How the hell did he know Talia was out there? Well, she did have a concussion. Maybe Blayk's ears were working better than hers.

He said, "See those large tweezers on the tray?"

"Yes."

"I want you to use them and pull the glass from her wound. That way I can have her artery clamped off faster," Blayk calmly explained. "Ready, honey?"

Rochelle wasn't sure if Blayk was asking her or his wife but gave a nod just in case.

"Now!"

Talia tugged the glass from her arm, and she yelped, but not with pain. She looked down and saw red covering her arm from elbow to inner wrist. Rochelle knew she shouldn't have looked but couldn't seem to help herself. Nausea roiled in her stomach when she saw flesh in the opening of her cut skin. She felt her eyes roll, and weakness permeated her body. She could hear the three Friess brothers talking to her, but nothing they said seemed to be intelligible.

Her head slumped against the table, and even though she could feel slight tugging where Blayk worked, she still felt no pain. Nonetheless, she felt as if she were drifting in and out of consciousness, and she had no idea how long it took for him to patch her up.

"Okay, I'm done. She only had a slight nick to the radial artery. I had to put in thirty stitches, so she's going to be sore and sorry for a while. Keep her arm dry, and if the pain gets to be too much, call me. And look out for any seepage."

Even though Rochelle heard everything Blayk said, it felt like she was hearing him from a long way off. Gentle, warm arms picked her up, and she tried to open her heavy eyelids to see who was carrying her but couldn't manage to. Just as the previous night, the slow rocking of being carried was enough to send her to sleep.

Chapter Four

Malcolm stared at his computer screen without seeing it. He wondered if there was any point in coming in to work today when his thoughts were still stuck back at the den.

It had been almost impossible to walk away from Rochelle, curled up and sleeping peacefully in their bed. Braxton was staying with her, and Malcolm knew his brother would make sure Rochelle was safe, but he still wished that he could be there, too.

Mate to two deputies and a sheriff, and we can't keep her from getting hurt. How could they, when Rochelle needed to be kept safe from herself? It was baffling.

A sigh rose up from the desk behind him. "How did she even live to be twenty-four?" Jarrod said.

Malcolm suppressed a grin as he spun his desk chair around. "Funny, I was just thinking the same thing."

His brother stood beside his desk, a sheaf of paperwork in hand. He was wearing a glazed expression that probably looked a lot like the one Malcolm was wearing today. "She's a hazard to herself." He dropped the papers on the desk and picked up the top sheet. He frowned at it, murmuring, "Tomorrow one of us will get to stay with her...Did you see this?"

"See what?"

Jarrod handed the page across. It was part of a report on yesterday's traffic accident out on one of the county roads. It had been something of a mystery. One vehicle, broad daylight, good visibility. The driver had been taken to the hospital, too battered for Malcolm or the others to get an account of the accident from him. He must have come around, though, because Malcolm found himself holding the man's statement.

The words jumped up in front of Malcolm's eyes. *Wolf darted into the road, forcing driver to swerve…*

"A wolf?" Malcolm looked up at his brother and found Jarrod's eyes cold and hard. "Shit."

Jarrod met his eyes and said telepathically, *"It can't be one of our pack. The Alphas wouldn't stand for this kind of thing."*

Malcolm checked over his shoulder in case there were any humans nearby, but they had the office to themselves. "You think this is related to the other incidents?"

Jarrod nodded silently.

That would make this the fourth incident in two weeks. The first three had been livestock getting mauled or disappearing. Local ranchers swore that they'd seen a solitary wolf prowling around their herds. Jarrod's official stance as sheriff was that there weren't any wolves in this part of the country. He said the rancher must have seen a coyote or a feral dog.

Of course, there were wolves, just not the kind that would go around harassing livestock.

"If it is a wolf," Jarrod said, breaking into Malcolm's thoughts, *"it has to be a rogue. No self-respecting* were *runs around causing wrecks and ripping the guts out of cattle."*

Malcolm dropped his attention to the paper in his hand. He knew how Jarrod felt about rogue wolves. His brother's position wasn't unreasonable, considering what had happened. Considering what lone wolves often meant in a community.

"Or just a coyote," Malcolm suggested.

"You always were an optimist." Jarrod picked up the phone from his desk. "Pull up those other reports from the ranchers. If there's a pattern, we'll find it." After a pause, he added silently, *"And don't mention the dead livestock to our mate."*

"Wouldn't dream of it," Malcolm muttered.

* * * *

Rochelle groaned as burning pain radiated through her lower arm. She moved her head on the hard, warm pillow beneath her cheek and whimpered when she moved her arm. *What have I done now!* Opening her eyes, she stared at the unfamiliar wall across the room.

"Are you in pain, darlin'?"

She jumped, which jolted her sore arm and caused her to whimper again. Lifting her head and leaning on the elbow of her good arm, she looked up to find herself draped over Braxton Friess. Her clumsiness that morning came rushing back with startling clarity.

"Oh shit," she whispered and then pushed off of Braxton to a sitting position. "I can't believe I did that."

"Don't move your arm too much, darlin'. You don't want to pull the stitches."

"God sakes, why do I have to be such a klutz?" she muttered, looking away from the sexy man lying next to her on the bed. He was so big it was a wonder his feet weren't hanging off the end of the mattress. But the bed must have been custom made, because he fit perfectly.

"I need to get going." She inhaled jerkily.

"No!" Braxton exclaimed. "You can't drive with only one arm functional and a concussion, darlin', that would be dangerous. Plus you need to be here so Blayk can keep an eye on your wound. You could get an infection."

"He gave me a shot of antibiotics. I'll be fine. I'll write you out a check to cover the cost of the damage I've caused." She scooted to the side of the massive bed. Standing made her go light-headed, and she couldn't see for a moment. Big, muscular arms wrapped around her waist, and when she could see once more, she was lying on the bed again.

"You are too weak to be up and about, Rochelle. You lost a bit of blood this morning and will need to take it easy for a few days," Braxton said, a frown marring his handsome face. "Don't be in such a hurry to leave, darlin'. You can stay here for as long as you like."

"That's very generous of you, but I've already imposed too much." Lifting her arm to express herself caused her to cry out with pain.

Braxton reached over her and carefully placed her arm on top of a pillow. "Don't move again, Rochelle. You're causing yourself unnecessary pain. I'm calling Blayk."

With his command still ringing in her ears, he rushed from the bedroom. Slumping back on the pillows, she closed her eyes, intending to rest her heavy lids for just a moment. She must have dozed off, because it felt like only seconds had passed before Braxton and Blayk were in the room.

"I'm going to give you another shot for the pain, Rochelle, but you have to stay here and rest. You're going to feel weak for a few days. You lost quite a bit of blood, honey."

She jumped when she heard a growl and looked over at Braxton. He was glaring at Blayk as if he wanted to pound on him. *What the hell is he pissed about? Maybe he doesn't want me here after all.*

"Um, thanks, but I should be going," she said and tried to hide her wince as the needle slid into her upper arm.

"You can't drive with the use of only one arm, Rochelle. And I can't let you leave since I am now your doctor. Just let Braxton and his brothers take good care of you."

Rochelle wanted to argue, but she could already feel the pain medication working its way through her bloodstream. The floating feeling was so nice, and the pain in her arm began to lessen. Giving in, she closed her heavy eyelids and slept.

* * * *

Braxton watched Rochelle sleep the day away. He couldn't bring himself to leave her alone, so he'd had Cindy bring up lunch and drinks. There was a jug of water and a glass sitting on the bedside table, ready for his mate once she woke. Glancing at the clock, he sighed with relief. Jarrod and Malcolm should be home any minute. He was going to need them at his side when they tried to convince their mate to stay.

He knew as soon as she opened her eyes she was going to want to try to leave. After pondering how to deal with a recalcitrant mate all day, he had decided honesty was the best policy. His ears pricked up when he heard his brothers coming up the stairs, just as his mate sighed and began to surface. *Perfect timing!*

Braxton poured a glass of water, ready to ease his mate's dry mouth as he watched her breathing change. She was so fucking gorgeous, and he'd been struggling with his wolf all day long. He was definitely going to have to go for a run later tonight. Hopefully by letting his beast run free and take control for a while, he wouldn't have such a hard time with his dominance over his inner animal.

She opened her eyes, and even though they were glazed from sleep, he felt as if he was drowning in her depths. A shiver raced up his spine, raising the hair on his nape. But that wasn't the only thing to twitch with desire. His cock jerked and filled with blood until his erection was pushing against the zipper of his pants.

He sat down on the side of the bed, slipped an arm beneath her neck and shoulders, and held the glass to her lips. She closed her eyes and sipped until she'd had her fill. Just as he placed the glass back on the bedside table, his brothers entered the room.

"How are you feeling, baby?" Jarrod came over to the bed.

"Fine, thank you."

"Glad to hear it," he replied and turned to look at Braxton.

"How is she really?" he asked through their mind link.

"Our little mate is very tired. She woke up in a lot of pain, so I called Blayk and he gave her another shot of painkillers."

"Good," Malcolm said from his position against the far wall. *"She hasn't said anything about staying?"*

"She's been asleep all day," Braxton answered. *"But Blayk told her she had to rest for a few days. I don't know if she will though. I think we should tell her what we are and what she is to us."*

"I don't know if that's a good idea. She may think we are crazy and take off," Jarrod replied.

"How the hell else are we going to make her stay?"

"Our mate needs to get to know us better before we tell her about us."

"Okay, agreed. But we have to talk her into staying until she's fully recovered. That will give us about six days for her to get to know us," Braxton stated.

"What are you doing?" Rochelle asked, drawing his eyes to her.

"Uh, we just…"

"Are you telepathic? 'Cause it looked like you were all talking to each other without actually speaking."

All three of them froze. Braxton was the first to recover. *"Fuck! How the hell are we going to get out of this?"*

"Tell her we are," Jarrod said.

He cleared his throat nervously. This was going to go over like a ton of bricks. "Yes, we are, darlin'."

Her eyes widened. "No way!"

Braxton exchanged a look with Jarrod. "Way," he said to Rochelle.

She examined him critically, as if looking for some outside sign of his telepathy. She examined Jarrod and Malcolm in the same way. Braxton tried to come up with some way out of this.

Then she said, "Wow. That is way cool. Are you triplets or something?"

Rochelle was gazing at them with a combination of awe and curiosity. This was not the freak-out Braxton had expected.

Malcolm answered, "No. But we are pretty close. We like to share. *Everything.*"

Rochelle crossed her legs as if settling in for a good story. "So when did you find out about your ability?"

"We've had it since we hit puberty," Jarrod answered.

"You can't read minds, can you? Are you empathetic?"

"No, darlin'. We can't read minds or feel what others feel." Braxton saw her shoulders slump as if in relief. Her eyes moved from him to Malcolm and Jarrod and then back to him again. When she wiggled on the bed, he caught a waft of her desire. Closing his eyes, he inhaled deeply, and his wolf pushed against him, wanting to claim its mate. Clenching his teeth, his pushed his animal back down, asserting his dominance.

God, how he wished he could assert his dominance over Rochelle. First he would strip her clothes from her delectable little body, and after he had tasted her mouth he would lick his way down until he came to her pussy. He would lap up her cream until she came and then do it again and again.

When he opened his eyes to look at her she gasped and her jaw dropped open. He curled his hands into fists and felt that his fingernails had changed slightly. She pushed up from the bed with her good arm, keeping her injured one close to her chest, and sat on her knees in the middle of the bed.

"Your eyes have changed. They are a glowing gold color. How do you do that? God, they look so pretty."

"Go, Braxton. Now!" Jarrod commanded through their link.

"No, wait," Malcolm said as he moved away from the wall, walking closer to the bed. *"Let's see how she handles this."*

"How are we going to explain that we can change our eye color?" Jarrod queried.

"Just tell her it's part of being a telepath."

Braxton cleared his throat while trying to wrest control of his wolf. His voice came out a little deeper and gruffer than usual, but at least it wasn't a garbled growl. "It's part of being a telepath, darlin'. Most of our family members have the same ability."

"Way cool. Is that why you all live together, so the general public doesn't realize what you can do?"

For a moment, Braxton couldn't do anything except stare at his mate in astonishment. Not only was she not scared of their abilities, she was thinking about how they fit into the way the pack lived together.

His desire for her mingled with a kind of awe. This was what it was like to have a mate, he realized. She was perfectly suited to them.

"In a way," Brax answered her. "We are a very close-knit family, Rochelle. We all like to live and work together. Each set of siblings and family unit have their own suite of rooms. We have lots of privacy, but we can also mingle when we want."

"That must be so nice." She sighed wistfully, glancing over to Malcolm and Jarrod. "How come your eyes aren't glowing, too?"

"Our eyes only glow when we have to concentrate really hard, baby," he answered, and Brax saw his brother's gaze run over Rochelle's bare legs and his nostrils flare as he inhaled her scent. If he kept that up, his eyes *would* be glowing pretty soon. Brax himself was only just in control of his wolf. Jarrod suggested, "Why don't I run you a bath? Or would you prefer a shower?"

"As much as I would love to soak in that giant tub, I think it's going to have to be a shower. I want to wash my hair."

"Okay," Brax said, moving toward the bedroom door. "I'll go and get a plastic bag so we can tape it to your arm. You have to keep that bandage and your stitches dry."

And I'll have an excuse to get out of here. He headed for the door before he even heard Rochelle's reply.

In the hallway, he stopped, breathing deeply. Now that he couldn't smell her desire as much, he could pull himself together.

It astonished him that Rochelle had accepted that they had strange abilities. Their little mate was a little quirky, but it worked to their advantage.

Braxton looked down at his hands and at the claws that were only now beginning to recede into his fingers. He hoped that Rochelle would be just as calm about the fact that she was surrounded by werewolves.

Because they were going to have to tell her soon. Braxton's wolf couldn't handle another second of this torture.

Chapter Five

Rochelle ogled Braxton's ass as he left the room, and her pussy clenched with arousal at such a damn sexy sight. She looked up to see Malcolm and Jarrod staring at her heatedly.

Quickly lowering her eyes to the quilt, she traced a pattern on the material and shifted into a more comfortable position. She caught a hint of musk from her wet pussy as she moved and hoped like hell they couldn't smell her desire.

Glancing up at them again from beneath her lowered lashes, she saw them still staring at her with golden glowing eyes. She was so fascinated she lifted her head to stare back. Jarrod inhaled and groaned as he closed his eyes. The muscles in his jaw were clenched and his hands were fisted. Malcolm seemed to have the same problem. As much as she wanted to scamper from the bed and enclose herself in the bathroom, she didn't want to move again in case they really could smell her wet vagina.

Movement near the door drew her attention and she watched Braxton walk toward her. He had a plastic bag and tape in his hands, and she reached out for them gratefully.

"I'll help you wrap up. Are you going to be able to shower by yourself?"

"Yes. I'll manage," she answered while he taped the plastic to her arm.

"We'll be back to escort you down for dinner." Braxton rose to his feet. "We have some things we need to do before we can eat. Just yell if you need help."

The three men left without a backward glance, and she relaxed for the first time since she had woken to find herself draped all over Braxton. *God sakes, girl, you need to get a grip.*

The shower was awkward, but she managed to wash, dry off, and dress. It would have been a lot easier to ask for help, but she had never been naked in front of a male before, and she wasn't about to start showing her body to strangers now. Yet she had to admit that she was intrigued by the lifestyle she'd glimpsed in this house. She wanted to know why all the couples weren't couples at all but were ménage a trois or ménage a quatre. It was the kind of arrangement she'd only ever read about in books, but what she wouldn't give to be part of such a big, close-knit family. What she wouldn't give to live that fantasy with Jarrod, Malcolm, and Braxton.

Rochelle would never dare ask any questions, but she was definitely going to watch the ménage members interact. Michelle, Keira, Talia, and Samantha seemed to glow from the attention their husbands bestowed on them. They had to be in love with the men in their lives. What woman would marry or hook up with more than one male if they weren't?

Rochelle had listened to the women she worked with bitching about the men they were either married to or in relationships with. Even though the married females had said they loved their husbands, they always managed to complain about something their men did or didn't do.

There was no way in hell she was getting into a relationship with a man unless she was certain she held his heart as much as he held hers. She had seen what happened to the children from broken and dysfunctional families or unwanted pregnancies. No way was she subjecting a child to what she had gone through.

A loud growl from her stomach made her realize she had skipped lunch. She was hungry and didn't think she could wait much longer for the three men to return to escort her down to dinner. She was just pondering whether it would be rude of her to go down by herself when she heard a snarling sound coming from outside the door to the suite. It sounded like a rabid dog was on the other side.

Just as she reached for the door handle and pulled it open, she heard a terrible snarling sound and Malcolm's voice as he pushed on the suite door. Looking down, she jumped at the sight of a large wolf in the house. In her hurry to get away from the beast, she tripped and began to topple.

There was nothing she could do. She yelled as the edge of the solid wood door slammed into her forehead before she could dodge it. Blackness formed before her eyes in little pinpricks, and she felt herself swaying on her feet. When her vision cleared, a worried-looking Malcolm stood before her with his hands on her arms, keeping her steady. Looking down when she heard another growl, she stared into the glowing golden eyes of a wolf. She tried to pull away so she could back up, but Malcolm still held her arms.

"Fuck!" Malcolm exclaimed. "Are you all right, honey? I'm so sorry. I didn't realize you were at the door. I was too busy growling at Braxton and didn't catch your scent. Get out, now!"

"What?" Rochelle asked breathlessly, still a little dazed from the knock to her head. Malcolm was looking at the wolf angrily and then turned back toward her when it left her sight.

"Are you okay? Shit. Blayk!" Malcolm didn't give her time to respond.

He scooped her up into his arms and ran for the stairs. Blayk met them halfway, and Malcolm told him what had happened.

"Look at me, Rochelle," Blayk demanded.

Shifting her eyes to him, she let Blayk check her pupil responses. "She doesn't have any lasting effects, but she's starting to bruise. Get her into the dining room and we'll put some ice on her head."

"I'm right here you know. You can talk to me," she said belligerently.

Malcolm carried her the rest of the way downstairs. "I am so damn sorry, honey. I didn't mean to hurt you. Let's get you seated and we'll get some ice."

Rochelle hid her face against Malcolm's neck as he carried her into the dining room. The conversations happening around the room ceased, and she just knew everyone was looking at her again.

Malcolm sat down and placed her on his lap. She sniffed against his skin and felt heat permeate her body. *God sakes, he smells so good.* Without thinking about what she was doing, she opened her mouth and licked the side of his neck. *Yep! He tastes as good as he smells.*

The body beneath her hardened, and a groan rumbled against her side. Rochelle gasped when she realized what she had just done. *Could you be any more geeky or obvious? How the hell am I going to be able to look him in the eyes after what I just did? Now it's definitely time to get back on the road.*

"Here's the ice pack," Blayk said from behind her.

"Rochelle, look at me, honey," Malcolm said.

She kept her face lowered, shook her head slightly, and tried to burrow into him.

"You have nothing to be ashamed of, honey," he whispered in her ear. "I would love to taste you, too. Now let me see your head. I don't want you to bruise or swell. Shit. Every time I look at you I am going to feel guilty for hurting you."

"It wasn't your fault." She finally lifted her head. "I always manage to get in the way or hurt myself. I'm just so clumsy."

"Fuck! You have a bruise already." Malcolm frowned. "Lean back against me and let me hold the ice to you head."

Rochelle did as he commanded and sighed as the slight throbbing began to recede.

"Are you okay, Rochelle?" Jonah asked.

"Yes," she sighed. "I'm fine. I'm always getting hurt somehow. Don't worry about it."

"We do worry about you, baby," Jarrod said as he sat beside them. "You always seem to be in such a rush. You need to slow down some, Rochelle. You won't hurt yourself then."

"I know. The nuns used to say the same thing."

"Nuns?" Braxton asked as he sat on her other side.

"I grew up in an orphanage," she answered quietly so the other people in the room wouldn't hear. Not that she was ashamed of her upbringing, but she didn't blurt out her life history to all and sundry.

Rochelle hesitated, realizing that her history was relevant, in a way. She hadn't told the brothers that she'd never so much as been naked in front of a man before, much less these three.

How would they react when they realized what a prude she was? That was what her roommate had called her, at least. She'd been called frigid, too. Although being called such names hurt, she hadn't been about to sleep with just anyone. Rochelle would be the first to admit that she'd gotten her sense of right and wrong from the nuns who ran the orphanage. Her female acquaintances were into drinking too much alcohol and having one-night stands. Rochelle had learned to respect her body. She had gone out with them a time or two, but when they had left her alone to hook up with men just to get laid, she had left and gone home again. Having sex just for the sake of it wasn't her thing, and being treated like a piece of meat by the opposite sex was just downright revolting to her. The nuns had instilled such a strong moral code into her she wondered if she would ever let any man touch her.

But she didn't feel at all frigid around these three men. She was so hot that she was all but melting. It confused the hell out of her, but it excited her, too. Never had she been drawn to men as she was to the three Friess brothers. She felt so strongly about them, and even though she hardly knew them, she knew she was in danger because of these feelings.

Why couldn't you be attracted to one man instead of three, girl? God sakes, what am I going to do when I have to leave?

"You're here now, that's all that matters," Malcolm stated.

She smiled at him, her thoughts moving backward. He'd said something weird a moment ago... "What did you mean about growling at Braxton?"

She felt Malcolm tense and looked up at him. He wasn't looking at her. He was looking at Braxton and Jarrod again. They had to be doing that telepathy thing again. *God sakes, how fantastic would it be to communicate without others hearing your conversation?*

"You're doing it again. Aren't you?"

"What's that, darlin'?" Braxton queried.

"You know. The telepathy thing," she answered quietly.

The conversations, which had resumed around the dining room, ceased once more. When she looked up, every eye was on her again.

Malcolm rose to his feet, taking her with him. He walked out of the dining room without a backward glance. When she looked over his shoulder, Jarrod and Braxton were following. They looked grim.

What the hell have I done now?

Malcolm entered the living room and sat on the large sectional sofa, once again pulling her onto his lap. He glanced up at Jarrod and then Braxton, and she could tell by the expressions on their faces that something serious was going on.

Did they want her to leave? She would, if that's what they wanted. But the thought of not being near the three Friess brothers caused sharp pain to pierce her chest.

God sakes, Rochelle, why did you have to come to care for them so quickly when no other man has ever gained your interest?

Chapter Six

Jarrod hadn't expected Jonah to command him to tell his mate what they were. But he had interrupted when he and his brothers had been communicating privately. They had been debating whether to tell Rochelle what they were when she had mentioned their telepathy again.

His cock was rock hard and had been since the moment he had inhaled her scent. It was a constant battle between him and his inner beast for control. And even though he won, he didn't know how much longer he could continue this way. But they needed to tell Rochelle what they were and let her decide if she wanted to stay with them.

"What's going on?"

"First of all, I want to know how you're feeling," Jarrod said as he looked her over with concern.

"I'm all right. My arm is a little sore and so is my head, but otherwise I'm fine."

"Blayk has advised that you stay here until you're completely healed. Are you going to do that?"

"I've thought about it, and the rest will do me good. I can't promise anything, but I think I can stay for a few days."

"Okay. But let me tell you that we would really like you to stay until you have healed. We would worry about you if you left beforehand. You were injured on our property, and we feel responsible for your injuries. In fact, we would like it if you stayed a lot longer."

Rochelle laughed and then sobered quickly. "You can forget about feeling responsible. I've always been a klutz. It doesn't matter where I go or what I'm doing, I always seem to find a way to hurt myself."

"You need to stop rushing everywhere, sweetness," said Malcolm. "You are in such a hurry to get where you're going you don't see what's in front of you."

"I know," she sighed.

"We have something we need to tell you, Rochelle." Malcolm shifted her on his lap until she was resting with her back against his arm and shoulder but could still see Jarrod and Brax. "I want you to listen without interrupting, and then if you have any questions, we will answer them. Just remember that we would never hurt you. Okay?"

Rochelle eyed Malcolm warily and then turned her gaze to him and Braxton. Brax was sitting next to him on the large coffee table in front of the sofa.

"You have seen our eyes glow and you know about the telepathy," Malcolm began to explain. "What you don't realize is that we haven't told you everything."

"We care for you very much, darlin'," Brax said and reached for one of her hands.

She opened her mouth to answer, but Jarrod said, "No. You need to let us explain."

Taking a deep breath, he reached for her other hand and looked at Malcolm as he wrapped his arms around her waist. The last thing Jarrod wanted was for his mate to panic and run away. First, she could end up with another injury, and as far as he was concerned she had far too many already. Secondly, he wanted Malcolm to restrain her in case she became hysterical.

Taking a deep breath, he exhaled slowly and took the plunge.

"We are werewolves, Rochelle. And you are our mate!"

She opened her mouth, but nothing came out. Her mouth snapped closed, and her breathing escalated. Malcolm pulled her in tighter against him, offering her comfort as well as keeping her from running.

Jarrod could smell her nervousness, but he didn't scent fear. That was something at least.

"W–What? What are you t–talking about?"

"Don't be scared, darlin'. We would never harm you," Brax reiterated.

"B–But there's no such thing as werewolves."

"We are living proof that there is." Malcolm hugged her tighter. "Brax, why don't you show her?"

Braxton rose to his feet and moved away from the coffee table. When he began to undo the buttons on his shirt, Jarrod heard Rochelle begin to pant. He wasn't sure if it was because she was nervous or turned on. Using his wolf senses, he sniffed the air and held in the grumbling growl forming deep in his chest. Their little mate was as aroused as she was scared.

* * * *

Rochelle couldn't believe what these three men had just told her. She thought she was the one who was a little eccentric, but they took the cake.

What the hell are they on? Suddenly she questioned her acceptance of their so-called telepathy. Yeah, they seemed to be able to communicate silently, and their eyes did change color, but how much was she expected to believe?

Why did I say I would stay for a few days? What am I going to do?

When Braxton rose to his feet and began to remove his shirt, she thought maybe they all had a screw loose. Yet she couldn't seem to tear her eyes away from the bulging muscles or the tanned skin he revealed. He was a sex god. His skin was a bronzed color, and she wanted to walk over to him and run her hands over his flesh. Cream leaked from her pussy and dampened her panties. Her nipples hardened and her breasts swelled.

Shifting her body only reminded her that she was sitting on Malcolm's lap. Heat penetrated through her clothes, causing her body to warm even more. A hard bulge was poking into her hip, and she didn't have to look to see what it was. Squirming again, she tried to move her body away from his hard cock.

"Shh, sweetness, you're safe with me," he whispered in her ear.

Yeah, that may be, but who's gonna keep you safe from me? Shit! I did not just think that.

Braxton's hand tugged at the button on his jeans, and then he slowly eased the zipper over his erection. Licking her lips to moisten their dryness, she watched avidly, not wanting to miss a moment. *God, I feel like I'm gonna come.* His hands moved to either side of his hips, and he hooked his thumbs into the waistband of the denim. She looked up and nearly melted from the heated, hungry look he pinned her with. *Take a few deep breaths, girl. You have to stay in control. They are a little crazy even if they are all sex on legs.*

No! Don't even think that. They are very nice men who have offered you a place to stay for a few days. Nothing more!

Then why did it feel like her heart would be ripped out when she left?

With slow deliberation, Braxton pushed his jeans down. His body was pure male perfection. She exhaled in a rush, which sounded more like a whimper than a breath. Braxton's cock was huge. Long, hard, and thick, it jerked slightly with every beat of his heart. Glancing up again, her gaze connecting with his, she stared deeply into his eyes. They changed from their normal color to a glowing gold. All of a sudden, the lines of his body began to blur and waver. His nose and mouth began to elongate, and he knelt down on the floor until he was on hands and knees.

Rochelle covered her mouth and watched with fascinated horror as the muscles in Brax's body shifted and undulated beneath his skin.

Terrible cracking and popping sounds resonated through the room as his form began to change. Just when she was about to push away from Malcolm and run, the noises stopped.

Standing before her, where Brax had been, was one of the biggest wolves she had ever seen. When he moved toward her, she squeaked and pushed back into Malcolm. Malcolm was speaking to her, and even though she understood every word, she couldn't have replied had her life depended on it.

"It's all right, Rochelle. We are still the same men we were before. We would never harm you, sweetness. Don't be afraid."

Is he for real? Of course I'm afraid. This sort of thing is fiction. Legend and mythology. This is not happening.

"Breathe in and out a few times, baby. Relax, don't be frightened," Jarrod said in a calm, soothing voice.

Braxton stopped in front of her. He was standing so close she could feel his warm breath through the denim of her jeans. As she stared at him, the fear she had been feeling slowly eased, and awe took over. *This shit is fantastic! How is this even possible?*

Without her permission, one of her hands reached out hesitantly toward the large wolf. She jumped when he chuffed in the back of his throat. She began to withdraw, but he moved closer and placed his large head beneath her hand. She rubbed his soft, silky fur, and a deep, satisfied rumble spilled from his canine mouth. With a nervous giggle, she reached toward his back and threaded her fingers into his fur. Using her nails, she lightly scraped them over his skin. He arched his back and rumbled with pleasure.

Slowly he moved back, and she scratched behind his ears before he pulled away completely. Standing clear of her, he stood completely still and stared at her. Once more the noises his body made as he changed caused her to cringe, but moments later he was back in his glorious, naked human form. With graceful ease he rose to his feet and began to re-dress.

"H−How is this even possible?" she stammered.

"Our father was a werewolf, baby," Jarrod explained. "The werewolf gene has been in our family for many generations. It goes back too far for us to be able to trace, but we only know that every male born into this family has the Lycan gene and we are all able to turn into wolves once we hit puberty."

"Does that mean that everyone who lives here is also a werewolf?"

"Yes, sweetness," Malcolm replied. "All the males can change into a wolf."

"Do the women change as well?"

"No," Braxton answered. "As far as we know there are only four women in the entire world who can change into a wolf. One of those women lives here with us."

"Who?"

"Keira," Jarrod responded.

"You said the males had the werewolf gene. If that's so, then how come Keira is a werewolf?"

She watched cautiously as the three men looked at each other. Even though their eyes didn't change color, she knew they were talking to each other. The signs were there in their body language.

"I'm not sure you're ready to hear that yet, baby," Jarrod said.

"I asked, didn't I?" Rochelle looked at them expectantly. She heard Malcolm sigh and looked up to see him nodding at his brothers.

Braxton moved back to the coffee table and sat down next to Jarrod. Jarrod reached for her hand and threaded his fingers with hers. Leaning down, he kissed the back of her hand, and she felt another gush of moisture leak from her pussy. Malcolm groaned, and she looked up to see him sniffing the air with his head thrown back and his eyes closed.

Oh shit! No, he can't, can he? She looked back at Jarrod and Braxton and saw them sniffing the air, too. *Oh. My. God. They can. They can smell my wet cunt. Well, they are werewolves, Rochelle, of course they can scent you.*

Looking down so she couldn't see the desire in their eyes, she asked, "Well, are you going to tell me how Keira ended up a werewolf?"

"Keira was shot and mortally wounded. The only way to save her life was to turn her," Jarrod explained.

"How?"

Braxton shifted, drawing her gaze, and he reached for her free hand. "Darlin', we don't change humans to werewolves unless it's absolutely imperative. It's too dangerous and very violent."

Malcolm leaned forward slightly and gently cupped her chin so she was looking at him. "We have to savage the human we are changing. In wolf form, we rip through the flesh and bite into organs. From what we have learned through generations, the Lycan gene needs to be embedded deeply so it can be taken into the human's body. There is no way of knowing if the person will survive the attack. That's why we don't do it. Keira was at death's door and unconscious when she was changed. She didn't feel any pain."

Rochelle felt her eyes widen, and her breath was panting rapidly through her lips. *What the hell have you got yourself into, girl?*

"Take deep breaths, sweetness," Malcolm said, brushing his thumb over her cheek repeatedly.

Finally her breathing evened out and she became aware of the tension in the room. Were they scared she would become hysterical? Even though her equilibrium was off kilter, she had never been the type to get frenetic. Rochelle's brain began to work at warp speed. She had so many questions and knew they would probably answer most if not all of them, but the most prominent one formed on her lips. And then the words Jarrod spoke previously ran through her mind.

You are our mate.

"What's a mate?"

Jarrod's voice caused her to turn back to him.

"A mate is a wife."

"W–Wife?" she squeaked. "Do you mean to all of you?" She then licked her dry lips as she awaited the answer.

"Yes, baby. You are the mate of Malcolm, Braxton, and me."

Oh fuck!

Chapter Seven

"No. No. No," Rochelle mumbled and then pushed off Malcolm's lap. He let her go, worried she would become even more frightened than she already was. Sniffing the air, he revised his opinion. She was more shocked and aroused than afraid.

"What are you afraid of, sweetness?"

"I−I…uh, shit."

"We would never force you do to something you didn't want, darlin'," Braxton said quietly.

"This"—she began waving her hand in the air toward them—"th−this can't be happening."

"What can't, Rochelle?" Malcolm asked, rising from the sofa. He slowly walked toward her, careful not to make any sudden moves.

"I can't be a mate," she answered.

Jarrod and Braxton both stood and made their way in her direction. She didn't back away, and that gave Malcolm hope.

"You are unequivocally our mate, baby," Jarrod avowed.

"How do you even know that?"

"We knew it the moment we scented you, darlin'," Brax explained. "Our wolves caught your fragrance and have been pushing at us to claim you ever since."

"Claim me?"

"We want to make love with you, Rochelle. And our wolves want to bite you and mark you as their own."

"Bite me?"

"Shh, sweetness, come and sit back down and we'll explain it all to you," Malcolm said calmly and reached for her hand.

"No. I'm fine where I am."

Malcolm knew that she felt safer with her back to the exit of the living room. He wanted to pull her back into his arms and hold her, but she obviously wasn't ready for any more affection from him.

"When a werewolf claims his mate, it's usually while making love to his woman," Jarrod explained. "Our canine teeth lengthen and we bite into our mate's flesh. From what I've heard it's not painful, but our DNA is transferred to the female, binding her to us and us to her. You would have enhanced senses, and you would heal more rapidly than the average human. Once we are mated we can't be apart from our mate too long. If she ever left after the mating mark and bond are made, then the mates would eventually die."

"So I wouldn't…*she* wouldn't become a werewolf?"

"No, darlin'," Braxton answered.

"Are all the women here mates?"

"Yes, Rochelle. Except for Angela and Cindy," Jarrod said. "Angela was good friends with our Alphas' mother, and when her husband died she was offered the position of housekeeper. She lives here now in her own suite of rooms with her daughter."

"Why don't we all go finish our dinner?" Braxton suggested. "You didn't get to eat any lunch, and we can hear how hungry you are."

"Okay," Rochelle replied, then turned and headed toward the dining room.

Jarrod caught her before she could go. "Now I have a question for you."

"And what might that be?"

"Will you stay here with us until you are completely healed and then give us two weeks to get to know you better?"

Rochelle took her time before answering, and Malcolm knew his brothers were waiting with bated breath for her answer as much as he was. Their body language said it all. Jarrod's jaw muscle was ticking and Braxton's hands were fisted, but to anyone who didn't know them, it would have looked like they were waiting patiently.

"Okay, I agree."

Malcolm exhaled quietly and felt the tension ease from his taut muscles. That was a start.

* * * *

The howling of wolves made Rochelle look up from her book. Alone at the kitchen table, she shivered and reached for her coffee. Both Jarrod and Braxton had gone out for a run after dinner, saying something about needing to let their wolves loose. They'd invited her to watch, but she wasn't sure she was ready for that. A little time by herself with a cup of coffee and a book was helping her settle her thoughts.

This all seems so surreal. It's like I'm living in a waking dream. Not only did her men turn into wolves, they were her mates. They wanted her to stay here with them forever.

Rochelle asked herself if she was ready to give up her carefree lifestyle. She had no plans aside from continuing her cross-country road trip. But the idea has lost some of its appeal since coming here. She'd been out on the road because of a sense that she was missing something in her life. Well, perhaps she'd found it.

But why did they have to be werewolves? She wrinkled her nose. *Why couldn't I have been claimed by some nice herbivores?* Imagining her sexy, dominant men as deer or sheep made her giggle.

"What are you chuckling about?"

Rochelle's breath caught as Malcolm strode into the room. He tossed his empty beer bottle in the bin.

"Nothing," she said, annoyed that her voice came out in a squeak. "Want some coffee?"

"No thanks." He retrieved another beer from the fridge. His gaze stayed on her as he cracked the top and took a swig.

Another howl came from outside. Rochelle shivered at the lonely sound. Her attention was on the darkness beyond the window, and she was startled when Malcolm said, "It's us unmated males who do all the howling, you know. All our lives, we've waited to find our mate."

He means they've waited to find me. Rochelle swallowed as Malcolm came over to the table. He pulled out the chair next to hers and sat.

"I used to imagine what our mate would look like," he said.

Feeling self-conscious, she curled a strand of hair behind her ear. "Were you right?"

He shook his head slowly, smiling a little. "Not even close. Turns out I don't have a very good imagination."

They'd hoped all their lives to meet her, Rochelle thought, but she hadn't had all those years of imagining her perfect men, not outside of daydreams. "Tell me about you," she blurted out. "I don't feel like I know anything about you or your brothers."

"What do you want to know?" Malcolm toyed with the beer. Rochelle watched his long fingers, imagining how they'd feel on her skin…*Girl, snap out of it.*

She took a sip of coffee to buy herself time. When she put it down, the words leapt out of her mouth before she could stop them. "How did Jarrod get that scar on his face?"

Malcolm's expression hardened. *Dammit, why can't you learn to keep your mouth shut?*

"Unless you don't want to tell me," she added quickly.

He softened ever so slightly. "No. It's okay. Better you ask me than him. He doesn't talk much about it."

Malcolm paused for a swig of beer. "Jarrod fought a rogue wolf a few years back. They were a pretty even match. The bastard grabbed hold of Jarrod's shoulder-length hair and swiped at his face with wolf claws. Normally we heal fast and don't scar, but that was a fight to the death. When our bodies have to heal a lot of injuries, sometimes we can't heal all wounds completely. Hence the scar on his face."

"He killed the rogue wolf?" Rochelle asked softly.

Malcolm nodded. "And he'd do the same again if he had to." He paused, apparently lost in thought. Then he continued, "Jarrod told us later that as he lay fighting for his life, he swore that if he lived, he'd shave his hair off and never grow it out again. Then no one would be able to use it against him."

Rochelle fingered her own long hair. "That's sad."

"Well, being sheriff and all, it doesn't hurt that he looks like a badass now. Intimidation can be an advantage." His smile faded as he looked at Rochelle carefully. "He'd kill me if he heard me say this, but he feels a little insecure about his appearance. He knows what the scars do to women—they're too scared to look him in the eye most of the time."

"I'm not."

"No," Malcolm said thoughtfully. "You never flinch from him, and you always look him in the eye when you speak to him."

Rochelle felt a little embarrassed. "I didn't do anything special," she said.

"No, I think it means a lot to him. And it means a lot to me," he added in a softer voice, "that you said you'd stay for a while."

She lifted her gaze to him. She had only to look into his green eyes before she felt like she was drowning in them. She became aware of how close they were sitting to each other. She could reach out and touch him if she only had the courage.

No sooner did she entertain that thought than Malcolm reached across and grabbed her hand. He pressed his lips to the soft skin on the back of her hand. His long eyelashes fluttered shut.

The simple gesture sent desire pooling in her belly. "How did you know I wanted you to do that?" she blurted. "I thought you couldn't read minds."

Malcolm looked up at her without letting go of her hand. "I don't have to read your mind, baby. It's written all over your face."

He pushed his chair back from the table and tugged her toward him. "Come here."

* * * *

Malcolm's wolf senses caught the leap of her heart and the way its beat picked up. Her breathing escalated until she was literally panting for breath. He let her see the desire he felt for her and watched as her cheeks turned a becoming shade of pink. She quickly lowered her eyes and licked her lips.

Malcolm nearly groaned out loud. He could just imagine that little pink tongue swiping over the head of his cock before she opened her mouth and took him in. As he inhaled, he opened eyes he hadn't realized he'd closed and breathed her in. The scent of her musk called to him, and his inner beast pressed at him as his muscles grew even tauter and his hard cock pulsed against the zipper of his pants.

Every time her gaze landed on him, his skin tingled and his cock pulsed. God, he wanted so much to strip her naked and explore her sexy little body. His wolf was continually pushing at him, but he kept control. Just.

He tugged at her hand. Rochelle stood and edged around the corner of the table. She stood still with her head lowered. Even though she didn't know it, her position was a form of submission, and his wolf rumbled with approval.

Her eyes flicked up to his once more, and she quickly lowered her head again, her hair falling forward, and he knew she was trying to use it as a shield against him. This had to end now. He couldn't take much more. His wolf had been at him to claim her the moment it had set eyes on her. If he didn't do something now, he was scared his animal would wrest control from him.

"Look at me, Rochelle." He cursed the sound of his own voice. It was so deep and gravelly he had to prevent a wince from forming on his face. Her head snapped up, and she looked at him in surprise.

Whether that surprise was from his command or his tone he wasn't sure, but he didn't really care. All he cared about was having his mate in his arms.

He pulled her close and then down into his lap. She sat in a sort of trance, her eyes huge and her breathing rapid.

He couldn't wait any longer. He took her mouth in a ravenous kiss. His tongue pressed for entry into her mouth, and she opened to him beautifully. His wolf howled and demanded more. Just a kiss wasn't going to be enough for him, and judging by the way Rochelle melted in his arms, it wasn't enough for her, either.

Malcolm forced himself to break the kiss. If he didn't stop this now, he wouldn't be able to call his wolf off. Grabbing her around the waist, he picked her up and placed her on her feet. Rochelle wove a little, watching him with an expression of intense surprise. Once again she began to ask, "What...?"

He only shook his head. His brothers had been right to go for a run. Staying with Rochelle, being saturated in the scent of her desire, would only drive him insane.

He walked to the back door. As soon as he was outside, he stripped out of his clothes and changed to his wolf form within two strides.

He ran and ran and ran. But no matter how fast or far he travelled, her scent was embedded in his soul. Finally he slowed, his muscles quivering with tiredness, and stopped to look up at the moon. His mournful howl was echoed back to him by other unmated males roaming the grounds.

Chapter Eight

The next morning at breakfast, Rochelle was buttering her toast when Jonah Friess stood up at the head of the table and called for quiet. The others at the table—other wolves, Rochelle had to remind herself—all fell silent before Jonah spoke.

"I would like all of you to welcome Rochelle Murphy as a guest of the Friess Pack. She is the mate to Jarrod, Malcolm, and Braxton, and while she is still deciding whether she will become a permanent member of our pack, I expect all of you to show her the utmost hospitality." He turned his attention to Rochelle. "Rochelle, as the pack's Alpha, and perhaps someday your Alpha, too, welcome to our home."

Rochelle felt herself blush as the huge table erupted into cheering and clapping. She felt a little embarrassed to be the object of so much attention, but it swelled her heart, too. She'd never had a family, and she loved the warmth with which the pack seemed to accept her already.

She waited until the table had quieted and her own thoughts had settled before she leaned over to Jarrod, who was sitting closest to her. "What's an Alpha?"

"The leader of the pack," Jarrod answered. He paused to crunch some bacon. Rochelle averted her eyes until he'd finished.

She was so conflicted about agreeing to mate with one man, let alone three, but also about how they were going to deal with her being a vegetarian. Did it embarrass them that she couldn't stomach eating meat? And how was she going to survive every meal when just the smell of the meat and seeing others eat it caused her discomfort?

Plus she was a prude, or so she had been told. How the hell was she going to make love to three men? It might work out if they only wanted her one at a time, but deep down she knew they would all want to touch her and make love with her together.

She had so much to figure out she wasn't sure what to do. But she knew one thing for certain. She wanted all of them. The more time she spent with them the deeper her feelings grew.

Jarrod's voice pulled her from her reverie. "We have three Alphas in our pack. Jonah, Mikhail, and Brock are the most senior wolves of the Friess Pack. But Jonah is the most dominant over all."

"What do you mean?"

"Jonah is the most powerful wolf in the pack," Braxton said from her other side. "He has the last say, and his word is Pack Law."

"That doesn't mean that our Alphas don't take suggestions and advice from the rest of us," Jarrod said. "In fact, Jonah and his brothers are very good Alphas. They always put the rest of the pack before themselves. But if there is any conflict and no one can agree on a resolution, Jonah can and will use his power to cease any arguments."

"What power?"

"Jonah has the ability to compel compliance just by using his voice," Jarrod said. "Actually, so do the Betas like us. Betas are second in command to our Alphas."

"We've only discovered recently that mated males can also use their voices to compel their mate's obedience," Braxton added.

Compel? That didn't sound good. "What..."

Jarrod interrupted, "The only time that any male has used that compulsion was when their mate's life was in jeopardy or they could be injured. We would never force a woman into doing anything they didn't want to do."

"Which brings us to a good question," Braxton said. "What are you doing today, sweetheart?"

If Rochelle leaned forward a little, she could see Malcolm on Braxton's other side. It was impossible not to think about the way he'd kissed her last night. She felt her face heating again as she thought about exactly what she wanted to do today with each of them.

She answered hastily, "I don't know. Can't I hang out with you guys?"

"We have to work," Jarrod said.

"We're the entirety of Aztec's law and order, you know," Braxton added with a wink.

"Too right we are," Jarrod grumbled.

Rochelle glanced between them. "Are you shorthanded?"

"Well, our dispatcher is pregnant. As of next week, she's gone on maternity leave. Which means, I'll spend most of the week hiring." Braxton made a face.

"Hire me." It popped out of her mouth before Rochelle could think it over, but for once she didn't regret her impulsive words, not even when Braxton's eyebrows went up and Jarrod's came together in a frown.

"Not a good idea," Jarrod said.

"Why not?" He'd taken another bite of bacon, though, so Rochelle turned her attention to Braxton. "I'm a fast learner, and I don't want to sit here doing nothing. I'll get bored."

"Hang out with the other women," Jarrod said. "They'll show you the garden."

Braxton chuckled. "Jarrod, what do you think is going to happen when they hand her gardening tools? She'll have knocked herself unconscious as soon as they hand her a rake."

"Will not!" Except she could kind of see that happening, too.

Malcolm leaned around his brother and said, "Same thing goes if she tries to go with Samantha to the club. No offense, baby, but I don't think you should go near a stove."

"All the more reason for me to come with you," she said firmly. "You can keep me from hurting myself."

She caught the look that passed between Malcolm and Braxton. They saw her point even if they wouldn't admit it.

She turned to Jarrod and pressed her advantage. "How much damage can I do to myself if it's my job to answer the phone?"

"The sheriff's department is *not* safe," Jarrod said firmly. "And that's final."

Rochelle narrowed her eyes at him.

Braxton sat back in his chair, chuckling. "Oh man," he said. "Now you've done it."

* * * *

An hour later, Jarrod pulled into his parking lot outside the Aztec Sheriff's Department with Rochelle in the passenger seat. She beamed at the building. Her new place of employment.

Braxton and Malcolm had been much easier to wear down than Jarrod. By the end of breakfast, she'd had both of them trying to persuade their brother that she would be helpful and that they'd feel better keeping her in their sights. Jarrod had threatened to pull rank a couple of times, but Rochelle could tell he didn't really want to leave her at the pack house while the three of them were working. He finally agreed to take her to the office on the condition that she slowed down and tried not to hurt herself.

True to that promise, Rochelle went about getting out of the four-by-four very carefully, but Jarrod caught her arm before she'd even opened the door.

"I don't want you leaving the office unless one of us is with you, Rochelle," Jarrod said. "There have been a few strangers in town, and until we know why they are here, I want you within our sights."

"Surely they're just people passing through. Why are you so worried?"

"There have been some weird incidents lately. Some…coyote or something."

"Coyote?" she repeated. "Not a *were*?"

"The only *weres* in Aztec belong to the Friess Pack. We don't tolerate lone wolves out here." There was something about his tone that told Rochelle not to press the point. Jarrod went on, "If you want to go out anywhere, you let one of us know and we'll come with you."

"Okay," she said. Since she had only just convinced them to let her work, she wasn't about to rock the boat.

Jarrod led her inside, introduced her to a very heavily pregnant Trudy, and then left for his office. Malcolm and Braxton went to their own desks to begin work.

By the end of the day, Rochelle had picked up the workings of the police radio and how to fill in the paperwork necessary for each 911 call. She was to work with Trudy for the rest of the week, just so the other woman knew she had a handle on everything.

There had been several calls regarding accidents, which Malcolm and Braxton had attended to, but other than that the day had been relatively quiet.

Just as they were packing up for the day, a man walked into the office and demanded to see the sheriff. Rochelle didn't like the look of him. Not that she could have said what it was about the man that gave her the willies. It was just a gut feeling. She let Jarrod know that a man calling himself Harold James wanted to see him.

She watched surreptitiously as Jarrod led him to his office before she went back to helping Trudy set up for the night dispatcher. Harold left Jarrod's office looking a little more than pissed off. As he walked past her desk, though, he slowed. It looked like he was sniffing the air. He turned and pinned her with his cold, dark eyes, and the grin he gave her looked more than a little malicious.

Rochelle stepped back even though he wasn't close enough to touch her and then cursed herself for showing any weakness in his presence. An evil gleam flashed in his eyes, and then he left the office.

"Are you ready to go, darlin'?" Braxton asked as he entered the office from outside. "Malcolm is waiting in the truck. Jarrod is going to be another hour before he can get away."

"Okay," she squeaked.

Brax walked toward her and studied her intently. "Are you all right, Rochelle?"

"Fine. I'm just a little tired." *And imagining weird things.* She must be getting used to hanging around *weres* if she thought people were smelling her.

"Come on, then. Let's get you home."

* * * *

Over the next week Rochelle became proficient at and more comfortable with her new job, and instead of Trudy doing the work, she did. Trudy was more than happy to let her take control. She hadn't seen any more of that creepy man, Harold, and even though she had wanted to ask Jarrod about him, she didn't. She figured she was just being paranoid. There had been no reason for her to take an instant dislike to a stranger.

Returning home on Friday evening, Rochelle joined the other women in the living room for a glass of wine. Malcolm and Braxton had gone out for a run. Even though she would have loved to go outside and watch them change into their wolf forms again, there had been other males with them, and one thing she was definitely not ready for yet was to see other men naked.

Looking down when she felt small hands on her calves, she smiled and reached out to help Stefan to his little feet. Stefan was the Alphas' child, and he was so cute she couldn't resist picking him up. He gave her a cheeky grin and then tangled his fingers into her hair, giving a good tug. Rochelle didn't mind though.

Keira was currently nursing her six-month-old daughter, Emma, and Talia was burping her two-month-old son, Riley, and she wondered if Samantha was pregnant, as she was sipping a cup of tea instead of drinking alcohol. Michelle had been mated to the Alphas for over two years and Keira and Talia for a little less than that. Samantha was still relatively new to the family, having been part of the pack for only six months. But all the women seemed to have become fast friends, and Rochelle envied them their close camaraderie.

The pack members doted on the newest arrivals to the family, and there always seemed to be someone willing to relieve the new mothers if they looked like they were flagging. She cuddled Stefan and gently removed her hair from his little hands, then proceeded to lift his top and blow raspberries on his tummy. The gurgling laughs he produced were contagious, and she found herself laughing along with him.

"Do you want children of your own?" Michelle asked, taking the seat next to Rochelle on the sofa.

"Maybe someday. I've always loved children, not that I've been around any since I left the orphanage."

The toddler in her lap reached for his mom. Rochelle passed him over to Michelle, feeling wistful at the sight of the baby with his mother. "I never thought I'd have a man of my own," she said to Michelle.

The other woman's eyes twinkled. "Or men."

Rochelle laughed, reaching for her wine to hide her embarrassment. She still wasn't used to talking about this. "Or men," she agreed. "I was too hell-bent on finding what was missing to even think about starting a family of my own…but I think that's what was missing."

She looked around the room, at the women and their babies. She couldn't imagine leaving. The idea of getting back in her car and continuing her road trip gave her an actual physical pain in her chest. *This is where I'm supposed to be.*

Keira spoke up from the other side of the room. "Can I ask you a question, Rochelle?"

"Oh, sure."

"Why are you vegetarian? Speaking as a werewolf, it's kind of hard to grasp."

Rochelle looked down at her lap. "The orphanage had their own stock, and they used to bring someone in to kill whatever unfortunate animal had been chosen for that week. I used to pet the animals and name them. It was quite a shock to find some of my pets missing. I learned very fast to stay away from the animals."

All the women looked sympathetic. "You probably shouldn't watch the men hunt, in that case," Michelle said.

Rochelle recoiled. "I certainly won't!"

The others laughed. "They don't ever catch anything," Michelle reassured her. "We buy our meat from the supermarket."

"Don't think poorly of us for it," Keira said. "Werewolves can't help it."

"I know." As repelled as Rochelle was by the idea of eating meat herself, she was getting used to being surrounded by wolves. There were plenty of other aspects of pack life that made it well worth it to live among carnivores.

Rochelle felt a frisson on the back of her neck. She glanced toward the living room door and saw Jarrod standing there staring at her. Rochelle had never been more grateful that he didn't have access to her thoughts than at that moment, though actually, it didn't look like he was looking at her, more like through her. Something was obviously on his mind, but she just gave him a smile of welcome. She suspected his thoughts were still at work. Her body responded to his presence. Her breasts swelled, her nipples hardened, and her pussy leaked.

Finally he really looked at her and gave her a wink and smile in return. Then he disappeared back into the hallway.

* * * *

Jarrod stood in the living-room doorway, staring at his mate. When she smiled at him he gave her a wink and smiled back. As much as he wanted to walk into the living room, pick Rochelle up, and carry her upstairs, he couldn't. With one last glance at Rochelle, he backed away and headed outside.

He went through the kitchen door and into the backyard, listening to the sounds of the others running and howling in wolf form. His own wolf wanted to be let out. Being close to Rochelle all week was testing the limits of his control. But he was still preoccupied with an incident at work earlier that week.

Harold James, a lone wolf, in his town. The man hadn't done anything yet, nothing that they could prove, but ever since he'd come into Jarrod's office, he'd been trying to figure out what the wolf wanted.

On the surface, James had come to request permission to work in town. It was a formality since James was in the Friess Pack's territory. But he hadn't acted like a humble young wolf seeking entry into a pack. In fact, he hadn't asked about the pack at all…

"I promise I won't cause any trouble in your pack, Sheriff Friess," James had said. *"All I'm asking is to stay in your town for a couple of weeks while I look for work."*

Jarrod had asked, "What sort of work are you looking for?"

"My main area of expertise is construction, but I'm willing to do anything to earn some much-needed cash."

"Define 'anything.'"

"Oh, nothing nefarious I assure you, Sheriff. I'm willing to work in the local bar. I'm down on money at the moment, so I can't afford to be too choosy."

"What pack did you say you belonged to?"

"I don't belong to any pack, Sheriff. As I have already told you."

Jarrod didn't like it. The bastard was too smarmy for his liking. He wanted nothing more than to kick this lone wolf out of his town. He'd told James that he had to run it by his Alpha before deciding anything. Of course, Jonah had told him to follow his instinct, and his instincts were screaming at him to throw James out of town.

But if he refused the man's request, James wouldn't leave. Jarrod felt certain of that, just as he was sure that James was the lone wolf that had been causing problems around Aztec for weeks. He just needed proof.

Jarrod sighed and rubbed his eyes. It had been a long, trying week. There was nothing for it but to wait for Harold James to expose himself as a criminal. And in the meantime to make sure Rochelle kept out of his way. Jarrod didn't want his woman anywhere near the bastard.

A soft, feminine voice pulled him out of his thoughts. Jarrod turned to find Rochelle standing in the doorway to the kitchen. The warm light caught the highlights in her hair. "Are you okay?" she asked.

"I'm fine." When he turned back to the kitchen and approached, she backed up, out of his way.

Something in his chest twisted. Women always did that when he walked toward them. "Need something?" he asked.

She shook her head. Jarrod shut the door behind her and looked at her. If he were smart, he'd go for a run and get his wolf under control. But he wasn't feeling smart. He wanted his mate, not to keep running away from her.

And she wanted him. He could smell her desire from where he stood. Jarrod suppressed a groan.

"Come here, baby," he commanded.

"What's wrong?"

"Nothing. Do as I say."

She moved the last couple of steps and cricked her neck to look up at him.

He put his fingertips beneath her chin to keep her face where he could see it and where she couldn't help but see him. "Are you scared of me?"

The indignant look on her face almost made him chuckle. His feisty woman wouldn't stand for that suggestion.

"No," she said. "Malcolm told me that you think that. But I'm not scared of you."

Reaching out slowly, so as not to startle her, he gripped her waist and slowly lifted her until she was at eye level with him. She gasped and placed her hands on his shoulders for balance. He could feel the heat of her hands through the thin cotton knit of his shirt and craved her touch on the whole of his naked body.

"What..." she began to ask, but he ignored the question. Moving an arm, he placed it beneath her ass so she was supported by his forearm.

"Wrap your legs around me," he demanded and was pleased when she again did as requested. Then with slow deliberation he lowered his head until scant millimeters separated their lips. Her moist breath washed over him, and he groaned when his mouth finally connected with hers.

One taste would never be enough. She tasted so sweet, and he wanted more of her delectable flavor. Slanting his mouth over hers, he pushed his way into her moist cavern. Tangling his tongue with hers, he groaned as her flavor exploded onto his taste buds.

Jarrod carried her over to the small, round timber table and slowly lowered her until her ass connected with the wood, still keeping their mouths connected. He withdrew his tongue and nipped her full bottom lip and then sucked the tender morsel into his mouth. Her whimper of need was music to his ears, and he shifted until their crotches were connected. His cock jerked, and he pushed his hips toward hers, rubbing his cock against her cloth-covered mound. He could feel the moist heat emanating from her pussy and knew he wouldn't be able to stop until he got a taste of her delectable cream.

With practiced ease, he found the hem of her shirt and slid his hand beneath the fabric. Smoothing his way up over the warm, silky skin of her belly, he didn't stop until he reached the underside of her breasts. He moved the last couple of inches until he cupped her delectable flesh in his palm. He used his thumb to strum her nipple through the lace of her bra as he moved his mouth to her throat.

Licking and kissing his way down her neck, he nipped the sensitive skin where her shoulder met with her neck, groaning in response to her mewl of pleasure. With dexterity he didn't really feel at that moment, he flicked the front clasp of her bra and caught her breast in his hand as it spilled from the confines.

Moving back from her, he withdrew his hand from beneath her shirt and grabbed the hem. A scant second later, Rochelle was bared to him from the waist up. He perused her body as he inhaled her fruity scent and her musky arousal. She was a goddess. Her eyes were closed and her cheeks tinged a pink hue from her excitement. Her long golden-blonde hair spilled down her back to lie in waves over the wood of the table. Looking at her breasts nearly made him spend himself in his jeans. They were so full that the weight of them made them lie low against her ribs. They were tipped with very dark nipples. Jarrod never would have guessed she had such beautiful, large breasts hidden beneath her clothes.

"Open your eyes, baby. I want you to watch me."

When her eyelids fluttered and finally opened, he pinned her with his heated gaze and moved closer.

He wanted her bare to his eyes, and he wanted to taste her sweet pussy now. Tugging on the waistband of her jeans, he popped open the button and slowly lowered the zipper. Pushing his thumbs under the waistband, he stepped back and pulled them down over her legs. When he reached her ankles, he cursed his eagerness that had made him forget to remove her shoes. Quickly remedying that, he then removed her jeans and panties. His hands shook with need as he reached out and touched her thighs. He was pumped up so hard he was scared he would hurt her with his zeal, so he was careful and lightly caressed her silky limbs from knee to hip.

A whimper from her drew his gaze upward, and he barely held it together when he saw the glitter of desire in her beautiful, hazy blue eyes. Snagging a chair by hooking his foot around the leg, he drew it in close and sat down. Smoothing his hands to the insides of her thighs, he gently parted her legs and stared at the soft, bare lips of her cunt.

Reaching down to her feet, he guided them to the table to spread her legs wide, giving him an unimpeded view of her pussy. Her clit was a protruding, engorged knot of nerves, her labia minora glistened with the dew of her juices, and he could see her cream welling in the hole of her vagina.

Pulling the chair in closer to the table, he kept his eyes on hers and dropped his head down. He swirled the tip of his tongue over the small bundle of nerves near the top of her slit and groaned when she gasped. The slight taste of her liquid desire wasn't enough to appease his hunger, so he slid his tongue down through her moist folds, gathered her juices on his tongue, and swallowed them.

When he reached her hole, he stiffened his tongue and thrust it into her pussy. She moaned and bucked up against him, but he was the one in control now. He placed an arm across her lower abdomen and held her hips still. Sliding his tongue into her as deeply as possible, he curled the tip and collected her cream. He growled with delight as he lapped her up and didn't intend on stopping until she had given him her all.

He shifted his free hand to her pussy and lightly rubbed the pad of a finger over her clit. The internal muscles of her cunt rippled around his tongue, and another gush of juices trickled into his mouth, but he still wanted more. Lifting his head, he peered up to see her lying flat on the table with her neck arched and her eyes closed. He was too intent on giving her pleasure to reprimand her for not watching him.

He rimmed her pussy hole with his finger and then slowly eased it inside. Searching gently, he growled when he found her G-spot and her pussy rippled around his digit. Bending down once more, he flicked his tongue over her clit and massaged her hot spot. She gripped his finger so tight, he could just imagine how she would feel around his cock.

Inserting another finger, he began to pump them in and out of her cunt, making sure to pass over her sensitive nerves. Her muscles clamped and released on him as he continued to bestow pleasure on her, all the while laving her clit with his tongue. Even though he still had his arm anchored across her hips, she rocked them to the rhythm of his pumping digits. Jarrod could tell by the noises and gasps she made that she was close to her peak. So he crooked his fingers, making sure not to take them off her G-spot, and gave slight tugs until she was writhing and sobbing with ecstasy.

Her breath hitched in her throat, the walls of her vagina clamped down on his fingers, and then she screamed. Her body convulsed around his fingers and she drenched his hand with a gush of her cream as she climaxed. Not letting up until the last contraction faded away, he slurped on her sensitive pussy until he swallowed all of her cum.

When she was done and her body was lax and supine with satiation, he lifted his head and withdrew his fingers from her pussy. He caught the glitter of her eyes beneath drooping eyelids.

Gripping her shoulders, he helped her to sit up and stared into the depths of her blue eyes.

His wolf picked up the sound of his brothers entering their suite after going for a run. It was time. "Yes or no, Rochelle?" he asked in a deep, gravelly voice.

"Wh−What?"

"We want to mate with you, baby, but bear in mind that if you agree, there is no turning back. You'll belong to us. Yes or no?"

As Jarrod waited patiently for her answer, his brothers came into the kitchen. He knew they had heard the question he had just put to their mate by the way they waited for her answer with bated breath.

Rochelle turned her head and looked at his brothers. Her cheeks got redder, but she didn't try to hide her sexy little body away from them. He heard her gulp and draw in a breath, and then she squeezed her eyes closed. Clenching his fists so he didn't pick her up before she answered, he rose to his feet and nudged the chair away.

Just when he thought he was going to have to walk away from her before he lost control, she gave a slight nod of her head.

Joy and love filled his heart, and his muscles primed even more as blood rushed through his body.

"I need to hear you say it, baby."

Chapter Nine

Rochelle couldn't believe she had just let Jarrod pleasure her with his hand and mouth. Even though she had just climaxed, her pussy pulsed with renewed need. All three men were looking at her for her response.

She had thought long and hard about whether or not to let them mate her and claim her. She'd thought about whether this would mess up her travel plans or if she wanted to keep traveling at all. The thought of never being with them caused shards of pain to pierce her heart, and she knew she couldn't leave. Somehow these three men had worked their way under her skin and into her heart.

All three of them had taken such good care of her when she had been injured. Their solicitousness and attention to her needs had slowly ingratiated them to her. Jarrod with his no-nonsense attitude and commanding personality made her dream of babies and making love, as did Malcolm with his caring attitude. Yet he could be dominant when he decided he wanted something, and so could Braxton with his easygoing but no less masterful nature. They were all so different, but they each seemed to fulfill a need in her she never knew she'd had until she met them.

Rochelle had learned more about herself in the last couple of weeks than she had in her entire life. She was submissive, and yet if needed she had more than enough backbone to stand up for what she wanted or believed in. Not once had they belittled her for not wanting to eat meat, and they were always looking out for her in case she was in danger of hurting herself. She felt so cherished when she was with them, and it didn't hurt that she would get a ready-made large family.

She had finally figured out what she had been searching for. Love, family, and acceptance. She had found that here with them. Three words hovered on her lips, but she wasn't sure if they were real or just an effect of being their mate.

She settled for the one word they were dying to hear right now. "Yes," she whispered on an exhalation.

Jarrod pounced and had her in his arms before her next breath. He rushed from the room. Rochelle wrapped her arms around his neck, placing her face close to his skin, and breathed in his intoxicating scent. Her gaze connected with Malcolm's and Brax's over his shoulder, making her pussy clench again. They were looking at her as if she were a starving man's next meal.

She lost sight of them for a moment when Jarrod carried her into a bedroom, and she looked around curiously, having never seen this room before. Her eyes snagged onto his as he placed her on a huge bed and followed her down. He kissed her mouth with none of the slow buildup he had used previously. The kiss was hot, wet, and wild and so carnal she felt as if she were on fire.

When he withdrew from her and pushed away, she shivered, goose bumps forming on her skin now his big, warm body was no longer covering her.

Gasping with awed desire, she noticed that Brax and Malcolm were standing at the end of the bed completely naked. They each had a hand wrapped around their impressive cocks, stroking the length of their shafts as they stared at her. Braxton's cock was longer, but Malcolm's was wider. She could see clear fluid glistening on the corona of each of their dicks. The two brothers both had ripped, muscular stomachs and torsos. Their pectorals flexed and their biceps bulged as they masturbated.

Jarrod's low growl drew her gaze, and she watched with heated fascination as he began to tug his tight T-shirt over his head. She couldn't prevent a whimper from escaping when she saw just how packed full of muscle he was. No matter how hard she tried, she couldn't seem to catch her breath. It seemed that whenever the three Friess brothers were near her, the sexual tension between the four of them was so thick that it squeezed all the oxygen out of the room.

Licking her lips to moisten them, she looked down to see Jarrod lowering the fly of his jeans. Her gaze connected with his when he rumbled out a groan.

"You keep doing that, baby, and I'm going to give you something other than your lips to lick."

"What?" she asked, totally confused. Instead of answering, he hooked his thumbs into his pants and pushed them off his hips. That the man didn't wear any underwear was the first thought to flash through her mind. She tried to pull her eyes from his body when she felt the mattress dip on either side of her but couldn't seem to manage such a feat. Knowing Malcolm and Braxton were now on the bed with her made her breathing accelerate even more.

With her eyes riveted to Jarrod's groin, she nearly came when she saw what he had been packing in his pants. He was a lot wider than his brothers and, if she wasn't mistaken, an inch or two longer. His cock curved up at the tip, and she wasn't so sure he wouldn't hurt her if he tried to push that huge weapon inside her.

Trepidation washed over her in waves, and she squeezed her thighs together with nervous denial.

"I won't hurt you, baby. I'll take you nice and slow the first time." Jarrod climbed onto the bottom of the bed.

Rochelle felt like prey to a predator as Jarrod crawled toward her on all fours. His eyes stayed connected with hers, and he gently ran his palms up her thighs. She squeezed her legs together more tightly, but she was no match for him. He slid his hands between her limbs and gently pried them apart just above her knees.

"I can smell your cream, baby. If you allowed it, I could spend hours drinking from that sweet pussy."

Rochelle closed her eyes on a whimper and tried to temper the urgent need she felt to be filled by him. Even though she knew what was to happen, she had no idea if she would feel pain. That made her even more anxious. When Jarrod growled low in his throat, she opened her eyes to stare at him. *Did I do something wrong?*

"Keep your eyes open, Rochelle. I need you to keep them on me," he rasped.

Jarrod shifted on the mattress, pushing between her legs and spreading his own. The position left her wide open for his viewing. Heat crept up over her face, and she knew her cheeks had turned a bright pink color.

"You have nothing to be embarrassed about, baby. I love looking at your pretty little cunt." As he spoke, he moved his body over hers, leaning on his hands but not touching her anywhere.

She wasn't sure how much more suspense she could stand. Without thought, her hands reached up and began stroking over his massive shoulders. He made a sound in the back of his throat, and she quickly withdrew them.

He reached out and ran his thumb over her bottom lip. It took everything in her not to snap at his digit with her teeth. Rolling her lips inward away from his touch earned her a hard pinch to her nipple.

Fire zinged from her nipple down to her pussy, causing her to clench and release more liquid out of her vagina, which trickled down to coat her ass.

"Look at me, Rochelle," Jarrod demanded in a raspy voice.

When she did as commanded, he leaned down and took her mouth. His kiss wasn't tentative. It was hot and carnally rapacious. The urge to close her eyes was strong, but she could see him watching her from beneath lowered lashes so kept her gaze on his.

Her body was on fire, and only these three men could douse it.

Jarrod pulled his lips from hers and moved back onto his haunches. He gripped her hips and pulled her closer.

"I'm going to fuck you and claim you now, baby," he panted, and she felt the head of his cock kiss against her dripping pussy. "Hold her arms above her head."

Oh shit. I've never done this before. Is this going to hurt?

Rochelle opened her mouth to voice those words, but Braxton caught her chin, turning her head toward him. His lips covered hers, and she moaned into his mouth, his tongue tangling with hers as Jarrod began to push inside her.

The flesh of her pussy stretched around the head of his cock. Burning pleasure-pain assaulted her senses, and she wanted to pull back and, at the same time, buck up to get more of his cock inside. He gripped her hips more firmly and she mewled into Brax's mouth with each gentle rock. She felt as if he was almost tearing her in half and couldn't prevent a groan of fear escaping. Brax removed his mouth from hers, and all movement stopped.

"How many lovers have you had, baby?" Jarrod asked.

Rochelle didn't want to answer because she already felt inadequate, but to not do so could cause her more pain than was necessary.

"None," she whispered.

"Fuck!" Jarrod growled and withdrew.

Oh God! I should have known this wouldn't work. Why did I say yes? I should have just denied them and left.

Tears burned the backs of her eyes, so she quickly lowered her eyelids. She couldn't bear to see their faces when she expected them to be full of disgust. Gulping in air, she tried to control her emotions, but the task seemed beyond her. The agony of rejection pierced her heart, and a sob escaped from between her lips.

"Rochelle, baby, what's wrong?" Jarrod inquired.

She couldn't answer. Never had she felt such humiliation and pain in her heart. Rolling to her side, she drew her legs up to her chest and wrapped her arms around her knees. Her whole body was quivering with unrequited desire and the agony of being pushed away.

Hands smoothed over her back in soothing caresses, but she didn't want their touch anymore. Lowering her head, she hid her face behind her knees.

"Did I hurt you, baby?" Jarrod asked in an anguished voice. "God, that is the last thing I wanted to do. That's why I stopped. I was going to get some lubrication to make it easier on you."

It took a moment for his words to penetrate her mind, but when they did, her tears slowed and eventually stopped. The room was quiet, but the three Friess brothers were still touching her in some way. There was a hand resting on her back, making soothing circles against her skin. Another was massaging the shoulder not pressed into the bed, and still another rubbed against the skin of her thigh and hip. Sniffling one last time, she slowly raised her head. Jarrod, Malcolm, and Braxton were all looking at her with wary concern.

"You didn't hurt me."

"Are you okay, baby?" asked Jarrod.

She gave a slight nod and pushed up until she was sitting on the mattress, her knees drawn tight against her chest. Still feeling vulnerable, she didn't want her nakedness to be on display.

"Why were you crying, sweetness?" Malcolm gently pushed her hair back from her face.

"I–I didn't think you wanted me anymore," she whispered.

Jarrod reached out for her, and before she knew what he was doing, he had pulled her onto his lap and his arms were wrapped around her.

"That is so not true, Rochelle. I'm sorry you thought that." He pulled her in tighter against his chest. "Your body was struggling to take me, baby. And since you're a virgin, I thought some lube would help the situation. Never, ever think we don't want you. That couldn't be further from the truth."

"Truly?"

"Yes, truly. Just wriggle those sweet hips of yours and you'll feel how much I want you."

Rochelle did just that. She shifted on his lap and felt his hard cock pulsing against her butt and hip. The man was huge. No wonder her body had struggled to accept him.

"Do you still want to do this, darlin'?" Braxton smoothed a hand up and down her arm. Turning toward him, she could see vulnerability in his eyes. Something she would never have expected to see from such a large, fun-loving, confident man. She turned the other way and saw that Malcolm was clenching his teeth and one of his hands into a fist. And then she realized that they were just as insecure as she was. Malcolm and Braxton were afraid of rejection.

Finally looking up, her gaze connected with Jarrod's. What she saw in his eyes caused her breath to hitch in her throat. His face showed what looked like love and acceptance but also resignation. He thought she was going to reject them, too. *How could I have gotten it so wrong?*

Chapter Ten

Jarrod had never felt so unsure of himself in his whole life. He had always been so confident and comfortable in his own skin. Human females often told him he was an arrogant, dominant asshole, but he knew that was just his wolf coming out. The knowledge that he had made his mate cry cut him to the bone. Never in his life had he envisaged this scene.

He had often dreamed of meeting their mate, but his wildest fantasies didn't even approach reality. She was such a pretty little thing, with her gorgeous blue eyes, full pink lips and long golden-blonde hair. Because she was so small compared to him, she made him feel his own masculinity. Never had he thought about how much stronger, taller, and more muscular he was compared to a female, until he had met Rochelle. Their woman made him feel like he could take on the world. But not right at this moment.

Drawing her eyes away from him, she looked back at Brax. She swallowed so loudly that he and his brothers clearly heard her gulp. Her little pink tongue slid out from between her teeth to moisten her dry lips. He exhaled in relief when she gave a slight nod. Emotion swelled in his chest. He felt humbled that she trusted them enough to let them continue to make love with her and claim her, and the tension he had been unaware of until that moment left his taut muscles.

"Are you sure, baby? I don't want you to feel pressured."

"I'm sure," she replied quietly.

"Look at me, Rochelle." He waited until her gaze met his once more. "I promise I won't hurt you, but if you feel uncomfortable at any time, all you have to do is tell us to stop. Okay?"

She nodded again and then drew in a ragged gasp. "Wait," she breathed. "How are we going to do this? You're not all going to…you know, at the same time?"

"Ah, baby. No. We'll love you one at a time tonight. But be reassured if you only want to take one of us tonight that that's okay."

Jarrod waited for an acknowledgement from her, and she nodded again. He nearly groaned when she licked her sweet lips once more.

Keeping his eyes pinned to hers, he slowly lowered his head. She didn't flinch away or look nervous, so he continued until their lips met. He started off gently, just brushing his lips over hers, letting her get used to his touch once more. Rochelle parted her lips, and he took her up on the invitation. Slipping his tongue into her mouth, he slid it along and around hers and sang Hallelujah in his mind when she moved and reached up to wrap her arms around his neck.

He lost himself in her when her fingers caressed up the back of his neck and then over his scalp. The sweet scent of raspberries and her musky arousal wrapped around him, and he didn't think he could wait much longer to claim her. Rising to his feet, taking her with him, he moved around the side of the bed and placed her in the center of the mattress. Jarrod was determined to set her on fire again before he entered her body.

Climbing onto the bed, his big body leaning over hers, he kissed his way down her neck, licking and nibbling as he went and making sure to linger on the erogenous zones he found on the way. Finally, with his mouth hovering over her beautiful chocolate-tipped breasts, he looked up at her. She looked like a sex goddess. Her face was flushed with arousal, her head was thrown back, and her chest was pushed up in silent offering.

Bending down, he took her turgid nipple into his mouth and suckled. She cried out, and her hips undulated in an erotic rhythm as old as time. Caging the hardened tip between his teeth, he flicked his tongue over the sensitive peak, over and over again. Rochelle writhed beneath him and whimpered with each pass of his tongue.

Releasing her nipple with a pop, he indicated to Malcolm and Brax to get back on the bed. They had moved away when he had carried her back to the center of the bed. Now he wanted them to help pleasure their mate.

"Watch her. I don't want her feeling any pain, but also give her pleasure," he said through their link.

Kissing and licking his way down her body, he watched from beneath lowered eyelashes as his brothers began to kiss and caress Rochelle. Braxton possessed her mouth with greedy sensuality while Malcolm sucked and pinched her nipples.

With a gentleness he was far from feeling, Jarrod smoothed his hands up her inner thighs, spreading her wider for better access. Lowering his head, he slid his tongue through her creamy folds and almost as far down as her anus. The sounds of pleasure she made as they stimulated her sexually were music to his ears. He laved and licked her until she was sobbing and arching her hips up continually. Reaching for the lubrication Malcolm had placed on the mattress, he coated his cock generously with the slick liquid.

"Watch her," he commanded his brothers as he moved up closer. Taking a deep breath to calm his raging arousal, he grasped the base of his cock and aligned it with her pussy. Malcolm was now kissing her while Braxton stimulated her nipples, but both his brothers had their eyes open and on their mate.

Grasping her hips, Jarrod slowly pushed his cock into her body. He groaned as her wet heat enveloped the head of his dick, and even though he wanted to surge in until he was as deep as he could go, he held still. Her body pulsed around his, causing him to grit his teeth. When the walls of her pussy loosened slightly, he rocked in another inch and stopped again. Sweat beaded on his forehead and rolled down his face as he fought to keep control.

Just as he was about to gain more depth, the little minx thrust her hips up at him and took more than he would have given her. She moaned with pleasure, and Jarrod sighed with relief that she hadn't hurt herself.

"Rochelle, don't move. I don't want to hurt you," he rumbled in a deep voice.

She pulled her mouth away from Malcolm and gasped. "More. Please! I need more."

"We need to go slow, baby."

"The lube's helped. It doesn't hurt." She groaned and looked at him with passion-glazed eyes. "I'm not made of glass. Fuck me!"

Jarrod began to rock his hips in a gentle yet consistent rhythm. With each forward move, he gained more and more depth. Her body was so tight that she enveloped him like a glove. As he retreated and pushed back in, she bucked up and took his whole length inside her. His balls were flush with her ass cheeks.

Now that he was fully embedded, his wolf wanted to claim its mate. His canines lengthened and his animal was pushing against him, but he pushed back.

Jarrod moved his arms beneath her legs and lifted, splaying her thighs wide. Her pelvis was tilted up, giving him easier and deeper access to her pussy. He pulled back until just his corona was resting inside her wet cunt and then advanced once more. With each thrust and rock of his hips, he picked up the pace until his cock was shuttling in and out of her wet vagina.

As he plunged back in he made sure his shaft rubbed against her clit and the head of his cock slid over her internal G-spot. Rochelle was sobbing each time he surged back into her pussy. Tingling warmth centered low against his spine, and he knew he wasn't far away from sexual gratification, but there was no way he was going over before his mate.

Reaching around her thigh, he found her clit and lightly massaged it with the tip of a finger. She cried out and the walls of her pussy rippled around his shaft. With one more surge he lightly pinched her clit between two fingers and grunted as she screamed out. Her whole body shook, bucked, and pulsed as she came. Cream bathed his cock, and he continued to finger her clit as he pounded into her twice more.

The liquid warmth spread from the base of his spine around to his cock and balls. His testicles drew up close to his body, and as he leaned over his mate and bit her shoulder, he roared with culmination. His cum spewed up his shaft and out the end of his cock. Rochelle screamed again as a second orgasm rocked through her.

Jarrod licked his claiming mark, bathing the wound with his healing saliva as he waited for his breathing to even out and his limbs to stop shaking. Using his hands, he smoothed the damp hair back off her face.

Never in his life had he felt so complete, content, and full of love. When he had bitten Rochelle, he had felt like a thread had connected her heart, body, and soul to his. He wondered if she had felt the same but didn't want to ask such an intimately emotional question. He wanted to tell her how much she meant to him but wasn't sure if she was ready to hear those three words yet.

Jarrod finally lifted his head and saw a contented, satiated smile on her face. Her eyes were closed and her body was limp with satisfaction. He kissed her tenderly and groaned when she responded by slipping her tongue into his mouth. Wrapping his arms around her, he rolled until they were on their sides and let her control the kiss. She finally weaned her mouth from his and looked at him with soft, hazy eyes.

"That was wonderful. Thank you."

"Baby, you are unbelievable. I should be the one thanking you. Not the other way around."

"Oh, but you made my first time so special. And I didn't feel any pain."

"I'm glad. Are you sore?"

"No."

Jarrod cupped her cheek and kissed the tip of her nose. He wanted to stay right where he was, but it wouldn't be fair to his brothers to continue monopolizing her attention. After another quick kiss, this time on her lips, he moved away so Braxton, who was sitting behind her waiting patiently, and Malcolm, who had moved off the bed entirely when he had blanketed her with his body, could have their time with her.

* * * *

Malcolm moved back onto the bed and lay down next to Rochelle. He cupped her chin and looked deeply into her eyes.

"Are you sure you want to do this, sweetness? Brax and I can wait if you don't want to."

"I'm sure. I want you both so much." Rochelle reached behind her in search of Brax, and his brother took her hand in his, leaned over, and kissed her shoulder.

"If it gets to be too much for you, darlin', all you have to do is say stop."

She looked over her shoulder. "Thanks, Brax, but I'm fine."

"You're more than fine, sweetness." Braxton waggled his eyebrows and smiled.

Malcolm was also smiling when he cupped her face and leaned in to kiss her. He groaned when she threaded her fingers into his hair and opened her mouth to him. She tasted so sweet and so right. It felt like he had been waiting for this moment forever, and now that it was finally here, he was a little nervous, but he pushed that from his mind and concentrated on Rochelle.

Tangling his tongue with hers, he then swept it around every inch of her mouth, along the insides of her cheeks, up to the roof of her mouth, and over her teeth. By the time he eased back and withdrew, they were both panting for breath.

Wrapping his arms around her waist, he pulled her in tight against his body and rolled onto his back. Her wet pussy slid over his engorged cock, and he moaned as his body pulsed with need. Using the strength of his arms, he helped her into an upright position so she was straddling his hips and he could reach her beautiful breasts. Keeping one hand on her rib cage to help her balance, he reached up with the other and began to knead one of her fleshy globes.

His little mate threw her head back and mewled with pleasure. The sounds she made wrapped around his heart. Never had he felt so connected to a woman before. Never had a female felt so right in his arms. He wanted to devour her inch by slow inch, but after watching Jarrod make love with her, he was barely keeping his rapacious hunger in check. His wolf was pacing back and forth, just waiting for the opportunity to claim his mate.

Slipping the hand from her ribs, he caressed his way down to her pussy. Sliding his fingers through her cream, he then began to massage her sensitive little clit. Her hips began to rock in time to his caresses, and fire erupted in his loins. He couldn't wait another moment. Malcolm had to have her, and it had to be now.

"Brax, help her," he demanded and cursed when he could hear some of his wolf in his deep, garbled voice. Braxton moved up behind Rochelle and lifted her up. Malcolm grasped his cock and held it away from his body as his brother lowered her back down. She was clutching Brax's forearms, digging her nails into his skin as she began to sink over his cock.

Rochelle opened her eyes and stared at him as she slowly took him into her body. Her mouth was open as she panted, and her pupils were so dilated they nearly obliterated her blue irises.

When she moaned, Malcolm reached for her hips and helped to rock her into a slow, erotic rhythm, up and down his erection. He held her still when he was halfway inside her, giving her body time to adjust to his penetration. Braxton was still behind her but was just bracing her now while he whispered into her ear.

"You are so fucking sexy, darlin'. I can't wait to make love with you. I can smell your pussy from here. I want to lick and suck on your pretty little cunt until I drink down all your juices."

Rochelle whimpered and then lifted up slightly. When she pushed back down, she didn't stop until her crotch met his pelvis. She had taken everything he had to give.

"Fuck! God, sweetness, you feel so fucking good. You're so hot and wet. I'm not gonna last long. Brax, help her over."

Malcolm gripped her hips and began to lift her up and down his hard cock. Braxton had an arm wrapped around her waist from behind and moved his free hand down to the top of her slit. Malcolm's balls were an aching mass of roiling cum and were slowly drawing up closer to his body. Planting his feet on the mattress for leverage, he thrust up hard and fast while continuing to control her movements. Rochelle's internal walls got tighter and tighter each time his cock slid into her pussy. She cried out as her sheath rippled around him, and then she screamed. Her cunt clamped down on his cock and continued to contract around him with orgasm.

Malcolm released one of her hips, pushed Brax away, and then wrapped his arms around Rochelle, pulling her down on top of him. He licked her shoulder and bit into her flesh, marking her as his. He howled against her skin as cum shot out of his dick, deep into his mate's body.

Malcolm held her tenderly as he licked his mating mark. Her body was lax over his, and she sighed as she snuggled into him. Running his hands up and down her back, he soothed her down from her climactic high.

He felt an invisible rope linking her to him and him to her. His days of feeling lonely were over. This deep connection to another person went beyond anything he could have imagined. Rochelle was the love of his life, the keeper of his heart and soul, and she didn't even know it.

Chapter Eleven

Rochelle's whole body felt like a mass of cooked spaghetti noodles. She didn't think she would ever be able to move again. It wasn't just physical pleasure that had knocked her flat but the sense of emotional connection she felt. The lovemaking she had shared with Jarrod and Malcolm had been out of this world, but when they had bitten her to claim her, she had felt as if she belonged for the first time in her life. She would never have believed that those special moments would feel so poignant and profound.

Her body was deliciously sated and her heart was so full. The urge to scream those three words as the two men claimed her had been so strong, she'd had to bite her tongue to stop them from slipping out. Maybe this was what she had been looking for all along, a place to belong, a place to call home.

Malcolm wrapped his arms around her waist and turned them both onto their sides. He kissed her lips and stroked a finger down her cheek as he gently withdrew from her body. When he moved away, she felt almost cold and bereft. She wanted to be surrounded in the heat of the three Friess brothers, and that scared her a little. Never had she wanted or needed to be near other people. The mattress dipped behind her, and she looked over her shoulder to see Brax looking at her hungrily.

"Do you feel okay, darlin'?" Brax rubbed a hand up and down her back with a look of concern on his face.

"Yes, I feel good." Rochelle rolled to her back and reached out a hand. He took it in his and kissed the back of it.

"Do you want a shower?"

She looked to Malcolm. He kissed her on the shoulder and smiled. "Go have a shower with Brax if you want to, sweetheart."

"Yeah, that sounds good."

Brax released her hand, leaned forward, and scooped her up. She wrapped her arms around his neck and leaned her cheek against his shoulder. For once, she was glad she didn't have to walk. She didn't think her legs would support her.

He carried her into the bathroom off her room and let her feet down to the floor, keeping an arm wrapped around her waist to hold her steady. Opening the shower door, he turned the water on, checked the temperature, and guided her into the large cubicle. Rochelle sighed with pleasure as the warm water ran down over her body. Warmth seeped into her lax muscles, awakening them enough so she could once more move without feeling like she was half-asleep.

"Come here, darlin', and I'll wash your hair."

He guided her under one of the many showerheads, and she wet her hair thoroughly. He pulled her out of the spray and massaged shampoo into her hair. The only time she'd had anyone else wash her hair was when she was a child and on the occasional visit to the hairdresser. But she loved having her hair washed and her scalp massaged. When he was done, he rinsed her hair and then picked up her bodywash. He sniffed the open bottle and smiled down at her.

"I always wondered how you smell like raspberries all the time. Now I know, and if you'll tell me where you get this stuff, I'll buy you a whole box full."

"I get it from the supermarket," she replied. They stood so close and Brax was so tall that she had to tilt her head back nearly all the way to look up at him. It hurt her neck if she stayed in that awkward position too long, so she lowered her head again.

He must have seen her dilemma, because he wrapped an arm around her waist and carried her a couple of steps to the built-in bench at the end of the cubicle.

"Stand up, darlin', and let me wash you."

Brax held her steady as she gained her feet. Once she had her balance, he stepped back and poured some bodywash into the cup of his hand.

"I can wash myself, you know," she said breathlessly while watching him work the soap into a lather.

"I know, but I like taking care of you."

Braxton began to run his soapy hands over her body. By the time he had finished, he had left no place on her untouched and her libido had turned from a low simmer to a raging inferno. He helped her down from her perch and guided her back under the spray

Once she was rinsed and dried off, he insisted on carrying her back into the bedroom. Jarrod and Malcolm were reclining on the bed, but she could see they had both used the other shower from Malcolm's still-damp hair and the few drops of moisture clinging to Jarrod's shoulders. They both moved higher up on the bed when Brax lowered her feet to the mattress.

"Are you still sure about this, darlin'? I don't want you to feel you have to make love with me. I can wait for another night, if you're too sore."

Her heart ached with emotion. Braxton reminded her so much of a gentle giant, and she knew he had meant every word he had spoken. She could see the sincerity in his eyes.

She reached out and placed her hands on his cheeks, then stared deeply into his eyes.

"I want nothing more than for you to make love with me, Brax."

He bent forward then and kissed her. He started off lightly, letting her get used to his touch. When she parted her lips on a breath, he slid his tongue into her mouth. She followed his lead when he deepened the kiss and tangled her tongue with his. He tasted different from his brothers, but his flavor was just as exciting and intoxicating. Rochelle moaned into his mouth, wanting the kiss to go on forever.

Reluctantly she withdrew her mouth to take gasping breaths of air. Braxton helped her to lie down on the bed, and Jarrod cupped her neck then placed a pillow under her head. She ended up with her ass on the edge of the mattress, her feet and legs off the end. Brax knelt down at her feet and rubbed his hands up and down her thighs. His intense, heated gaze connected with hers once more.

"Darlin', I want to taste your sweet little pussy. Just lie back and relax."

"Oh," was all she could manage to get out before he swooped down and devoured her. He ate her pussy like he was starving and would never get enough of her. How he thought she could relax when he was doing such exquisitely carnal, pleasurable things to her body was beyond her.

Arching up into his mouth, she mewled and sobbed as he laved the tip of his tongue over her sensitive clit. Then he slid that muscle down between her slick folds and thrust it into her pussy. Copious amounts of cream leaked out of her vagina with each stab of his tongue. When he brought his fingers into play, she thought she would die from too much pleasure.

The bed dipped on either side of her, but she was too caught up in the bliss being bestowed on her to take much notice. And then she was surrounded by masculine heat and hard bodies. Jarrod and Malcolm began to suck, lick, and pinch her nipples just as Braxton pushed two fingers inside her dripping pussy. It was too much, and yet she knew she would never be able to get enough of them. She threw her head back and screamed as waves of climactic rapture washed over her. The walls of her pussy spasmed with contractions until finally the last pulse faded away.

Opening eyes she hadn't even realized had been closed, she watched as Braxton rose to his feet. Instead of sliding her up the mattress as she expected, he sat down on the edge of the bed beside her and picked her up. He brought her over his lap, her legs straddling his hips as she faced him.

"Take me inside you, darlin'. I have to feel your pussy squeezing my cock."

"Oh God," Rochelle moaned. He held his penis steady for her, and she slowly lowered her body down.

They both groaned as her pussy enveloped his hard, hot flesh, and even though she wanted to slam down on him until he was all the way inside, she was feeling a little tender and took things easy. She clutched at his shoulders as she rocked up and down his hard shaft, letting her wet sheath adjust and moisten the way for his penetration.

When she was finally sitting on his lap, his penis embedded deeply inside her cunt, she held still for a moment, just savoring the sensation of having his cock inside her. He flexed inside her, and she mewled with delight and began to move up and down on his rod. It felt so good that she increased the pace until the sound of her ass cheeks slapping against his thighs resonated throughout the room.

Braxton helped guide her rocking motion by holding on to her hips, and then Jarrod and Malcolm moved to sit on either side of them. Each of them reached over and began to pinch her hard nipples once more. Zings of sensation raced down her body and pooled into her pussy, making her muscles clench and release, which only seemed to enhance the friction of Brax's cock shuttling in and out of her pussy.

Her womb began to feel warm and heavy, and her pussy began to ripple around his dick. Molten, liquid heat ran through her body, from her womb over her clit and pussy, and radiated out to her limbs. She curled her toes as tingles coursed up and down her legs, and then, suddenly, she was on the precipice.

Crying out as the pleasure became almost unbearable, she tilted her head to the side when Braxton licked her shoulder. She knew what was coming and sobbed as she got closer and closer to the peak. And then she was there, hovering on that cliff, waiting for the explosion that would send her hurtling off the edge.

White-hot erotic pain bit into the flesh of her shoulder, right next to where Malcolm had marked her. That pleasure-pain sent her screaming. Her pussy clamped and released around the cock buried in her vagina as she flew up and over the cliff into nirvana.

She was only vaguely aware of Brax's shout of completion, and then she slumped down against him, her body still racked with the occasional spasming aftershock. The same connection she had felt with Jarrod and Malcolm snapped into place, like invisible bands which led from her out to each of her men. Her heart was full of love, hope, and joy, which threatened to spill out of her mouth without her permission. But she held back, not quite ready to admit her love to them. She would bide her time, and when she felt it was right she would tell each of her men that she loved them. For now she was just content to snuggle with Braxton.

His gentle hands were running up and down her back, and he kissed her head. She opened her eyes when she heard movement and saw Malcolm heading toward the bathroom. Moments later, water was running into the large tub.

Her men took care of her. They carried her to the bathroom, washed and dried her again, and then she was in bed with three big bodies surrounding her. She counted her blessings. She had never thought to have one man care for her, let alone three.

She was content and happy for the first time in her life and just prayed to God that nothing and no one would jeopardize their relationship. As far as she was concerned she was now theirs and they were hers. God help anyone who got in between them.

Chapter Twelve

"Jarrod, how was work?" Jonah asked.

Jarrod stood in the doorway to the Alphas' office, still wearing his uniform. He'd come straight up here when he reached the pack house.

"Quiet, for a change, but we may have a problem."

Jonah swept a hand out to indicate Jarrod should sit down. After getting comfortable, he looked up to see both Mikhail and Brock entering the room.

"Explain," Jonah demanded.

"You remember that guy Harold James who showed up in town a few weeks ago?"

"The wolf looking for work," Mikhail filled in.

"He says that, but I don't see him working anywhere. I've had some of the Omegas looking out for him, but he doesn't seem to have gained employment. There are plenty of construction jobs around town that he could sign up with," Jarrod said. "One of the local ranchers saw James walking around down by his fence earlier today. The rancher went to shoo him off and spoke to him for a moment. It was definitely James. A couple of hours later, the man found dead sheep down where James had been. Eviscerated."

"He didn't see James shift, did he?" Jonah asked.

"No, but he suspects James anyway. I don't think James is being careful that humans don't see him shift, either. Something's wrong with that wolf." Jarrod paused. "I don't have enough evidence to arrest him for destruction of property, but my instincts tell me he's bad news."

"You can't arrest him under human laws, but Pack Law is another story." Jonah nodded. "Your instincts are usually correct, Jarrod. When you see James again, you may tell him I have denied his request to stay in our town. Do you want me to send more reinforcements with you?"

"No. I can handle the bastard." Jarrod felt relieved. He wanted this lone wolf away from his pack and his mate. His mate in particular.

"Okay, I'll leave him to you and your brothers then."

Jonah sat back in his chair. "How is your mate settling in? She hasn't done herself any harm in the last couple of weeks."

Jarrod gave a bark of laughter when Jonah smiled. "Rochelle seems to have slowed down some since she's been here. She's not rushing around anymore and she's fitting in quite well."

"Your mate has a warped sense of humor," Brock said with a grin. "She fits in with the other women just fine."

"Are you going to marry her?" Mikhail questioned.

"We're already mated. Why would I need a puny piece of paper to tell me we belong together? You and I both know that when we claim a mate, it's more binding than the human wedding ceremony."

"Yes it is. And we know that, but our women are human. With the exception of Keira, of course. Marriage is important to human society, so don't discount how she would feel about a wedding."

"Hmm, you have a point. I'll have to discuss it with Malcolm and Brax." Jarrod rose to his feet and walked toward the door.

"If you need help with anything, Jarrod, all you have to do is ask."

"Thanks, Alpha."

"Wait up, Jarrod," Brock called, and he halted in the hallway. "Are you going for a run? I thought I'd join you."

"Let's head on out then. I want to be back in half an hour. Dinner should be ready by then, and I'm starving."

"Did you ever ask Rochelle why she has an aversion to eating meat?" Brock led the way out back and began to strip his clothes off near the line of trees in the back garden.

"Umm, no."

"What are you going to do when she gets pregnant? You and I both know she is going to crave rare meat for the pup."

"I have no fucking clue," Jarrod mumbled and frowned as he, too, removed his clothes. He didn't even know how Rochelle felt about children. *Everything happened so fast.*

"If I were you, I'd inform her before it happens. She's such a feisty little thing, and if she doesn't give in to the cravings, she could get sick. The baby will just take all the nutrients it needs from the mother, but if she doesn't replenish her body, well, you get my drift."

"Shit, why does she have to be so complicated? You didn't have any trouble with your mate."

"Now, that's where you are wrong. We had plenty of trouble with Michelle, and she is just as single-minded as your mate is when she has a notion, if not more," Brock said. "Just remember that all the women who have ended up as our mates are no pushovers. They are all different in a lot of ways, but when push comes to shove, they can all be as stubborn as hell. I don't think they would be our mates if any of them lacked backbone."

Jarrod reached for his wolf and let his human side draw back. Moments later he ran amongst the trees. His animal howled at the moon, expressing the joy he felt as the cool night air ruffled his golden wolf pelt. He called to his brothers and quickly changed direction when they called back. Nothing compared to running free in the night, letting his animal have control for once. His wolf senses took over, and he sniffed the air, catching the scent of a rabbit. He took off after it, and even though he had no intention of killing the small creature, his beast reveled in the tracking and the chase.

He turned away, letting the frightened animal hide once more, and went to meet his brothers. They were already heading back toward the house. Brock was still out with the other wolves, and even though he could have kept running for hours, Jarrod wanted to shower and change before dinner. He loved spending time with his family at meal times, but he loved having Rochelle sit beside him more. She gave as good as she got, and he loved listening to her and watching how her quick mind worked. His little mate was a joy to be around.

She was teased often about being a vegetarian and her earlier clumsiness, but she took it all in stride. He just hoped she wouldn't be too sickened by the thought of eating meat once she conceived. They were going to have to talk to her very soon about the need to eat meat when she was pregnant. The last thing he wanted was for her to ignore the natural cravings of an expectant mate.

* * * *

Rochelle sat frozen in the garden. She had taken up her seat on the bench among the trees late in the afternoon and had settled down to read her book. Only when she'd heard Jarrod's voice had she realized how late it was. Her first inclination had been to jump up and go say hello to him and Brock.

Then she'd heard her name.

Now the men had moved off. She heard the yips and howls of wolves running elsewhere on the property, enjoying a run before the sun went down. Rochelle still sat where she was, their conversation replaying in her mind.

She is going to crave rare meat for the pup...

She covered her mouth and breathed deeply, trying to stop herself from gagging. Just the thought of eating any type of meat was enough to make her feel sick.

But if I have children with them, I'll have to.

It seemed clear that Jarrod had known as well as Brock had that this would be an issue. Why hadn't they told her?

Rochelle put down her book and began to pace. As Brock had pointed out, none of her men had ever asked her about her vegetarianism. Maybe if they had, they'd have realized that this was going to be a problem.

She walked around the outside of the house, not really taking notice of where she was headed. When she reached the carport, she realized that she wanted to go for a drive. She needed to clear her head.

All the men of the pack had their own place to park their vehicles, and most of the time they left the keys in the ignition. Malcolm's truck was no different, and since her car was blocked in, she couldn't get it out of the carport. She walked toward the truck. Without stopping to think, she got into the driver's seat, pulled the seat forward so she could reach the pedals, and turned the key. Moments later she was cruising down the driveway.

She wasn't running away, she just needed some time alone to process the new information. Even though she felt queasy, she was also angry and more than a little hurt that her mates hadn't deigned to tell her what to expect if she conceived their child.

They had never asked her why she didn't eat meat. That thought made her think that maybe she wasn't as important to them as she thought. She had asked them so many questions about their heritage, their wolves, and their childhoods she felt like she knew them inside out. Although she knew she still had a lot to learn about her men, they had more to learn about her.

Was she that inconsequential to them? Sure, they had asked her about where she was from, what she had done before she arrived in Aztec, and about the years she had spent in the orphanage, but they had merely touched the surface.

What the hell was she supposed to do now? There was no fucking way she was going to eat meat.

Calm down, girl. You're not even pregnant.

She sighed. But she wanted to have their children. They hadn't talked to her about that, either.

Maybe that was the problem. Maybe they didn't bring it up because they didn't see her having their kids…

"Whoa." Rochelle hit the brakes. In the deepening dusk, she saw the outline of a large animal by the side of the road. It was the wrong shape to be a dog.

It looked like a sheep. *Did someone hit it?* She slowed further, craning her neck to see. It wasn't moving, but she knew she couldn't just keep driving. The thought that it might be lying injured and in pain would bother her all night.

She pulled the truck onto the shoulder, the tires crackling on twigs and leaves from the trees by the road. It was darker in the shade, closer to night than dusk. After she slammed the truck door, the air was utterly silent.

Rochelle got two steps toward the sheep before she heard another sound. Something panted and moaned in the trees.

She stood still, peering into the darkness. There was something lying on the ground, further back from the road. Another moan and a cough was enough to get her feet moving again.

"Hello, are you okay?" she asked. She got close enough to see that it was a man. He lay on his side under the trees. Rochelle knelt down and reached for the man, intending to help him.

He moved so fast she was on her back pinned to the ground before she could draw breath, and his hand was covering her mouth. She couldn't even scream for help.

The evil gray eyes of Harold James stared down at her.

What is he doing out here? She hadn't seen the creepy guy since that day in the sheriff's office. He'd looked a little off kilter then, but now he seemed maniacal. His eyes stared down at her without reason, and there were twigs and leaves stuck in his hair.

Though she struggled to breathe under the pressure of his hand, she recoiled as his rank breath washed over her. "The pretty girl from the sheriff's office," he crooned. He sniffed. "Their mark is all over you."

She twisted, trying to get free from his hand, but stilled when she felt something sharp at her throat.

An evil smile warped James's face. "I'll put my mark on you instead."

His eyes began to change color and turned into a glowing gold.

Oh fuck. He's a deranged werewolf.

His mouth and nose elongated into a snout, and claws erupted from his fingertips. They dug into her cheek and pierced her skin. Blood dripped from the wounds, down over her jaw and onto her neck.

White-hot agony erupted through her body just after he bent his head. Pain such as she'd never known before burned into her neck where his teeth bit into her. She raised her arms and tried to fight him off, but she didn't stand a chance. He was way too strong and seemed to relish the pain he was causing her. Her eyes widened in horror when he lifted his head and stared down at her. Blood dripped from his mouth, and he snarled out a laugh.

Rochelle could feel lethargy creeping over her body as blood seeped rapidly from her neck. Her eyesight began to dim and her body shivered uncontrollably, growing colder with every beat of her heart. She realized that she was bleeding out.

Oh God, please help me. I don't want to die.

Chapter Thirteen

"Where's Rochelle?" Jarrod asked as he strolled into the dining room. Dinner was in full swing, but there was no sign of his mate.

"I thought she was out in the garden," Malcolm replied.

"Michelle might know," Brax answered.

Jarrod moved around the table until he was close to his queen. "Michelle, have you seen Rochelle?"

"Um, I saw her leave about ten minutes ago."

"Leave? Leave for where?"

"I don't know. She took one of the trucks." Michelle glanced between Jarrod and his brothers, watching them from further down the table. "She looked upset, but she took off before I could talk to her. I don't even think she saw that I was nearby."

"What's going on, baby?" Jonah asked as he sat next to his mate.

Jarrod slowly realized what might have happened. "Malcolm said she was in the garden."

Michelle nodded. "She went out there to read this afternoon, on the bench by the back door."

It was only a theory, but Jarrod's instincts told him that Rochelle had heard him talking to Brock. If she'd been in the trees, he wouldn't have seen her. And, distracted as he'd been by what Brock was saying, he wouldn't have smelled her.

In any case, she was gone. Alone. With that lone wolf James skulking around town.

"Fuck!" Jarrod growled, dread forming in his gut.

Jonah rose to his feet and snarled at Jarrod. "You will not talk to my mate that way."

Even though his profanity hadn't been directed at Michelle, Jonah didn't know that. Jarrod lowered his head in supplication.

"I'm sorry, Michelle, Jonah. I wasn't swearing at you. Please forgive me."

"Understood," Jonah sighed and sat again.

Jarrod sniffed the air after Jonah sat once more. "Do you have any idea why Rochelle was upset, Michelle?"

"No. Maybe she just needed some time alone."

Jarrod bowed his head to his Alphas once more and turned away. He raced from the room and gestured for his brothers to follow. *"We have to find Rochelle. She's missing."*

Jarrod picked up her scent and followed it out to the carport. He immediately noticed that Malcolm's vehicle was missing.

"Where the hell would she go?" Jarrod snapped. *"Take the truck. I'll track her in wolf form."*

He shifted. His senses were more powerful in this form, and as soon as his paws hit the pavement, he could smell lingering traces of exhaust. She couldn't be far ahead.

Jarrod raced up the drive, hearing his brothers starting the truck behind him.

He ran full tilt up the road, keeping the scent of the truck in his nose. Malcolm and Brax stayed close enough behind so that Malcolm could see him. *"There are more behind us to help search. Rylan, Tarkyn, and Chevy took over from Justin, Roan, and Chet after Jonah accepted them as Betas, and they began helping with the pack security and the real estate side of things,"* Brax said. *"They are coming from the other direction. They were just leaving the Aztec Club. If they see her truck, they'll stop her."*

"Good." He wasn't about to refuse help, but getting Rochelle to stop for them wasn't what worried him. He feared that she might already have stopped.

His gut was telling him she was in trouble. A rank, rotting odor reached him, and he put on a new burst of speed.

He saw the truck at the same moment that another vehicle pulled off the road beside it. He saw three men burst out, and he recognized the scents of Rylan, Tarkyn, and Chevy. Behind him, Malcolm pulled the truck onto the shoulder. Jarrod didn't slow down until he reached the trees where the others had gathered, knowing his brothers would be close behind him.

The sight that met his eyes nearly caused his legs to buckle. Rochelle was lying in a pool of blood, the side of her neck was gouged open, and her stomach had bite marks everywhere. He saw red.

Rylan, in wolf form, had cornered Harold James against a tree trunk. Jarrod didn't stop to question the fucker.

He had his prey in his sights, and nothing was going to stop him from taking it down.

Stalking forward on all fours, he kept his eyes on James and then leapt. He was so enraged he didn't even care when claws slashed into his side. *Kill* was the only thing that ran through his mind.

They circled one another. Jarrod waited for an opening. James jumped at him first. His claws slashed at Jarrod's side, and his teeth bit and tore at the scruff of Jarrod's neck.

Jarrod broke free. Rylan snarled and paced forward as if to join the fray, but Jarrod snapped his jaws at him.

"He's mine."

He had to keep his head in this fight. He wouldn't let memories of the other fight, the one that had nearly killed him and left him with his scar, intrude on his thoughts now. Not when his mate needed him.

Jarrod ignored the pain in his neck and circled his opponent again. James's attack was disorganized. This was a wolf who wasn't accustomed to fighting his own. But Jarrod was.

He darted close and grabbed hold of James's hind leg and crunched down hard. James howled with pain as the bone snapped.

Jarrod released James's leg. The injured wolf turned, hobbling. His eyes flashed gold, utterly empty of all emotion except for rage.

He leapt at Jarrod, but he was weakened and thrown off balance by his injury, and Jarrod was ready for him.

With a lightning-fast move, he side-stepped James's blow and then went in for the kill. His teeth sank into his opponent's neck, and he clamped his jaw together. Shaking his head back and forth, he growled and snarled until he tasted victory.

Finally he let James go and spat blood from his mouth. James was dead. He would never be a threat to his woman again.

Jarrod changed back into human form. Heedless of his nudity, he ran to where his brothers were trying to stop the blood from seeping out of his mate. She was so pale and lifeless that he feared they were too late.

"She's got a pulse. It's weak and thready, but it's there. Blayk is on his way with his van," Brax whispered.

Jarrod knelt down. His fingers couldn't find a pulse, but using his wolf senses, he could hear her heart stutter. She wasn't going to make it. Looking up at Rylan, who was standing a few feet off to the side, still in wolf form, he pleaded to him with his eyes.

"Rylan, you have to change her. She's dying."

Rylan whined and took a step forward. He sniffed Jarrod's mate and angled his head as if he, too, was listening to Rochelle's stuttering heartbeat.

"Please?"

"I want you and your brothers to back away from your mate." Rylan licked Rochelle's cheek as if trying to get her to wake, but there was no response.

"How long before Blayk gets here?"

"He's here, and so are the Alphas," Malcolm replied.

Jarrod looked up as Jonah, Mikhail, Brock, Blayk, Chris, James, Tarkyn, and Chevy entered the trees. The three Alphas immediately stepped forward. Chris took hold of Jarrod's other arm as Tarkyn helped to hold back Malcolm and Chevy helped with Brax. They were going to have to restrain them so Rylan could turn their mate.

As soon as Jarrod and his brothers were restrained, Rylan struck. He growled and snarled as he ripped into Rochelle's stomach, going deep into her organs. Her body convulsed, and Jarrod howled as he tried to control his wolf. The howls of his brothers joined his. He tried to snap at Jonah, but his Alpha just shoved his arm further up his back, asserting his dominance as Jarrod tried to pull away and go to his mate's aid. Claws erupted from his fingertips, and he could feel fur beginning to sprout from his skin.

"Jarrod, Malcolm, Braxton, control your beasts," Jonah said in a deep voice full of compulsion.

Jarrod immediately felt his beast quiver and shake as his Alpha's powerful voice washed over him. Not once had he taken his eyes from his mate, and he snarled one last time as Rylan stepped away from Rochelle, allowing Blayk to get to work.

When he had his wolf under control, he nodded to Jonah and Chris and watched Blayk intently.

"She's lost a lot of blood. I'm hooking her up to saline, and I'm also going to give her a pint each of your blood. As soon as I have her stabilized, we'll get her into the van and head home."

Once Blayk had the IVs in her hand and arm, he attached heart monitors and hooked her up to an ECG.

"Her heart's weak, but she's holding her own. Let's get her onto the stretcher and head home." Blayk gently pushed a back board under Rochelle. With Chris's help, they got her onto a portable stretcher and into the back of a van they used for emergency situations. "There's only enough room for one of you."

"Go," Malcolm and Brax urged him. He gave his brothers a nod of thanks and followed Blayk into the van. They were heading home moments later.

Jarrod took hold of Rochelle's hand and sat up near her head so he wouldn't be in Blayk's way. He watched as his cousin gave her a shot of painkillers as well as antibiotics and then began to clean her wounds with saline and antiseptic. James was driving the van, and even though he was speeding he kept the van from jolting too much. It was the longest ride of Jarrod's life.

Just as the van slowed and turned into the driveway of the pack house, Rochelle moaned, and then her body began to convulse. Jarrod had never been so scared in his life and began to pray. He didn't even realize he was crying until one of his tears fell onto his hand and rolled onto Rochelle's.

"This is normal, Jarrod," Blayk said. "Don't give up yet."

Taking a deep breath, Jarrod tried to push his emotions back and concentrated on his injured mate. The van stopped right outside the clinic at the back of the house, and with Chris's help they wheeled Rochelle into the office. All the time he pulled the stretcher, he had a hand on her shoulder so she wouldn't fall off as her body tried to accept the wolf DNA into her system. It took another ten minutes before her body stopped convulsing.

Blayk gave Rochelle another three pints of blood and more painkillers, and finally his mate's body began to heal. He could see the wounds closing right before his eyes, and he knew in that instant that she was going to be all right. Movement in his peripheral vision prompted him to lift his head, and he saw his brothers' pale faces. How long they had been in the room he had no idea. But when he saw them take a deep breath, he knew they had to have seen her struggle for life, too.

"Your mate is going to be just fine." Blayk confirmed Rochelle's condition. "Why don't you all pull up a chair and talk to her. I believe Keira said she heard every word her mates spoke to her when she was going through the change."

Jarrod was grateful to be able to sit down. His legs felt weak and shaky, and he knew he was in a bit of shock. He hoped to never have to see his mate in such pain again. Being careful not to jolt the needle in the back of her hand, he wrapped his fingers around hers and squeezed lightly. As he sat there trying to ascertain why she had left the den, he kept coming back to thinking she must have heard him and Brock talking about her craving meat if she became pregnant. At least that was the only scenario he could come up with for why she may have been upset enough to leave.

"Rochelle, I'm sorry we didn't tell you that you would crave meat if you got pregnant. I didn't mean to keep such a thing from you, it just never entered my mind. I have been a wolf my whole life, and since I've never had a mate before, I forgot to tell you something important. I hope you will find it in your heart to forgive me."

Using his free hand he smoothed the hair back from her face and bent down close to her ear.

"I love you, baby. Please, get better soon. I can't live without you, Rochelle. I was so lonely before you came charging into our lives. You are my heart and soul, and I will never let anyone hurt you ever again. If you can hear me and forgive me, please give me a sign."

Jarrod gasped when he felt one of her fingers twitch on his skin. He looked down at their joined hands and then back to her face.

"You can do it, baby. Come on, Rochelle, squeeze my fingers."

A slight pressure gripped his fingers for less than a second, but he knew that she forgave him. Tears of joy ran down his face, and he didn't care who saw him falling apart. Nothing mattered to him more than his mate.

Malcolm, who was sitting on the other side of Rochelle, moved his chair in closer to her and leaned over to kiss her cheek.

"I love you, sweetness. I'm sorry for our oversight, too. We didn't mean to forget. We are just so set in our ways that I guess we made some mistakes."

Malcolm looked up at Jarrod and then Braxton, and a slow smile spread across his face. "She squeezed my hand. You're going to be just fine, sweetheart. We're going to take good care of you."

Braxton moved from his place at the end of the bed and nudged Jarrod from his chair so he could get closer to their mate. He wrapped an arm around the top of Rochelle's head and leaned down to kiss her on the lips.

"You just rest, darlin'," Braxton said quietly. "We want you to take all the time you need to get well again. And when we have the all clear from Blayk we are gonna spend a whole weekend loving on you. You've filled up the emptiness that was in my heart, darlin'. You are the most precious thing in my life. I love you, Rochelle."

Rochelle moaned slightly and licked her lips, but her eyes remained closed. Jarrod had never heard a sweeter sound. He looked over to Blayk and watched as his doctor cousin checked his mate's wounds.

"Her wounds should be fully closed in another hour or so," Blayk explained. "She will sleep a lot, so don't get upset if she doesn't wake up until tomorrow or the day after. It will take a full week before she is feeling normal again. I will keep her hooked up to the saline until she is awake. We don't want her dehydrating."

"I think we should organize a temporary sheriff to take over until our mate has healed," Malcolm suggested. "I don't want her out of my sight again."

"I'll see what I can do, but I can't promise anything, Malcolm. I don't want to leave her side either, but we are the law of this town and we have a duty to others as well."

"I'll be perfectly fine." Rochelle projected her thoughts into their private mind link for the first time. *"You don't have to sit at my bedside and watch me sleep."*

"Rochelle? You should be resting, baby, not talking to us."

"I am resting. It's not like I'm doing a jig."

"Your mind needs to rest as well as your body, sweetness," Malcolm said.

"I won't be awake long. I can already feel myself floating. What happened to Harold James?"

"He's dead, baby."

"Because of me?"

Jarrod could feel her distress, and he hurried to reassure her. "It wasn't your fault, baby. He was out of his mind. We should have driven him out of town long ago."

"But then he might have hurt someone else…" He could feel her drifting off toward sleep, but she asked, *"I'm going to want to eat meat now that I'm a werewolf, aren't I?"*

"You don't have to if you don't want to, baby. We can get Angie to order more vegetables and fruit in for you, but your wolf may crave meat sometimes. Don't worry about it now, Rochelle, we'll work out an alternative," Jarrod replied.

Rochelle explained why the thought of eating meat was repugnant to her. "No wonder you were a vegetarian." Brax frowned. "You don't have to worry about that around here, honey. There have to be alternatives we can find for you, but we'll look into it later. You just rest and concentrate on getting well."

"Good, because I really don't think I could ever eat meat. Maybe I can get Angie to look at getting some of the vegetarian meat alternatives in, such as tofu, and if that's not enough to satisfy my and the baby's bodies, I'll have to look at something else. There's just one more thing I need to tell you all," she said, and Jarrod could hear the weariness assailing her.

"What's that, baby?"

"I love you all, too."

Jarrod looked at his brothers and knew the stupid grin they wore on their faces was mirrored on his own.

Everything was going to be just fine.

Chapter Fourteen

It took a full seven days for Rochelle to recover, but when she did, she was so full of vim and vigor she wanted to yell out loud to the sky. Even though Jarrod, Malcolm, and Brax hadn't wanted to leave her side, they hadn't been able to get anyone to take over the office for them, so they had taken turns going to work and staying with her.

The whole pack had come to visit her while she was recuperating, and the women had even brought her some chocolate from their secret stash, making it a game by keeping their gift a secret. Or so they thought. Blayk had come in just as she popped the last piece of chocolate into her mouth, and even though he didn't say anything, he had sniffed the air and given her a wink and a grin as he took her vitals.

It was a full moon tonight and also the first time she would change into a werewolf. Keira was sitting beside her on the sofa in the living room, and even though she appreciated the company, Rochelle was feeling a little restless and finding it hard to concentrate.

She looked up when Keira took hold of her hand. "It's not as bad as you're imagining, you know."

"God sakes, I feel like I'm about to throw up."

"You'll be fine. The only pain you will feel is a bit like growing pains. Once your wolf takes over, you are going to feel so free. It's an amazing experience."

"Everyone is going to see me naked, aren't they?"

"No one is going to ogle you if that's what you mean," Keira explained. "They are more interested in following scents and playing as well as tracking prey."

"God sakes, I don't want to do that, Keira. Just the thought turns my stomach. I don't think I can kill anything that lives."

"Who said you have to? Stop worrying so much. Just let your wolf take over and enjoy the experience."

"Do I have to…you know?" The thought of having sex with her men while in wolf form excited her, but she was also nervously apprehensive.

"You only do what you want, Rochelle. No one will force you to do anything you don't want to."

"Even my mates?"

"Especially your mates."

"Are you talking about us, baby?" Jarrod asked as he entered the living room.

"God sakes, I keep forgetting you guys can hear everything. Nothing is sacred anymore."

Jarrod sat down next to her and pulled her onto his lap and whispered for her ears only, "Now, that's just not true, baby. I promise we won't take you in wolf form if you don't want us to."

"Truly?"

"Yes, truly. And you don't have to hunt if you don't want to. We would never make you do something that makes you uncomfortable. You should know that by now."

"I do," she said on a sigh. "Sorry, I'm just a little nervous."

"You have nothing to be afraid of, Rochelle." Malcolm leaned down and kissed her cheek. "We will be with you every step of the way."

"Come on, let's go eat. I'm starving." Brax headed for the dining room.

"You're always hungry." Rochelle giggled.

"What can I say? I'm a werewolf and have a fast metabolism."

"I can't believe how much food you all eat, and that goes for me, too, now. I have never eaten so much food in my life. I am going to get fat."

"You don't have to worry about that, baby. Your weight won't change from what you weigh now. The only time you will gain weight is when you are pregnant, but you'll lose any excess fast. Michelle was back in her jeans within a week, which made her very happy, so I'm told."

"Oh, goody. The thought of being fat while pregnant doesn't bother me, but having to carry extra weight around for months afterward is just downright mean," she said in a garbled voice. "Jarrod!"

"Don't panic, baby. That was just some of your wolf coming out." Jarrod leaned down and kissed her on the lips. He stroked a palm up and down her back in a soothing, calming motion. "Are you ready to go to dinner?"

"Okay."

Jarrod stood up, but he didn't let her go. He carried her into the dining room. When everyone smiled at her, she felt her cheeks heat but smiled back. She loved the way her mates had looked after her over the past week.

They'd brought her drinks and food when she was in the infirmary, and Jarrod had even given her a sponge bath. When she had been allowed back into their suite, her men had each taken a turn spending a full day with her and seeing to her needs. What she treasured the most were the nights when she was surrounded by their warm, masculine bodies and she felt so safe and contented. Her men were careful not to bump any of her healing injuries even after she felt perfectly fine. They had been so solicitous and loving, she often felt tears of love and happiness prick the back of her eyes.

Jarrod lowered her into her seat but didn't sit down beside her. She glanced up at him curiously and then to Braxton, who was seated on her other side with Malcolm next to him. The scrape of chairs on the tile floor drew her attention, and she looked around the table to see everyone else rising to their feet.

Jonah tapped his wineglass lightly with a spoon to get everyone's attention.

"Tonight is a night for celebration. We welcome our new wolf sister, Rochelle, to the pack and hope you enjoy your first of many changes to your animal form. This dinner is in your honor, Rochelle. May you live long and have lots of pups."

Rochelle smiled and thanked everyone and watched with awe as Angie, Cindy, and the other women began to bring in platters of food. They were piled high with roast beef, lamb, and pork, as well as platters of steaks and some vegetables. Although the scent and sight of meat no longer made her feel queasy, she still couldn't bring herself to eat any of it. Maybe one day in the future she wouldn't remember the animals she had come to care for when she was a child, but until then she would continue to get her nutrients from her fruits and vegetables.

She'd also done some research while convalescing and had found a local farmer who treated his animals really well and killed them in the most humane way possible. She had decided that if she craved meat and had to eat it while pregnant, then she would ask Angie, the Alphas, and her men to buy their meat from that farm. Rochelle figured if she had control over where the animals came from and they'd had a good home, then maybe she could eat it if and when necessary.

Once dinner was done, everyone made their way outside to the rear garden. It was a bit disconcerting when people began to strip out of their clothes. She looked up at Jarrod, Malcolm, and Braxton, not wanting to see anyone else naked.

"Are you ready, darlin'?" Brax asked, placing his hands on her shoulders.

"I don't think I'll ever be ready."

"You'll be fine, sweetness. We won't leave your side." Malcolm took hold of one of her hands.

"Let me help you, baby." Jarrod moved in close and began to unbutton her shirt.

Once she was naked she watched in awe as her men undressed. *God sakes, they are so hot. And they are all mine.*

"We certainly are, baby." Jarrod smiled at her.

"God sakes, I can't believe you heard that. Get out of my head."

"We aren't in your head, sweetness. You broadcasted that thought loud and clear." Malcolm took hold of her hand again. Braxton moved in close behind her and wrapped an arm around her waist. She looked up at the moon and scratched the skin of her arm.

"Don't scratch, baby." Jarrod took hold of her other hand. "It's just your wolf you're feeling. Watch me, Rochelle, and call to your wolf. Don't fight it. Just relax and let go."

Rochelle kept her eyes on Jarrod's and watched as they changed to a glowing gold. She moaned when the itch spread over her body but didn't try to scratch this time. Braxton helped her to kneel on the ground, and Jarrod followed her down.

"That's it, darlin', let that pull drag you back."

Rochelle felt the nails of her hands and feet lengthen, and when she looked down she saw fur racing out along her limbs. It was the same color as her hair. Muscles twitched and bones cracked and popped, causing a deep ache in her bones, but the pain wasn't unbearable. She looked up to see Jarrod standing before her on all fours. He was absolutely magnificent. His fur was two shades lighter than hers, and she could just imagine what he would look like with hair.

Her eyes skittered to the side, and she took in Malcolm. He was nearly as big as Jarrod in wolf form, but his coat was a light brown. Turning to Brax, she noted his fur was lighter than Malcolm's but darker than Jarrod's. All their eyes were that glowing gold color.

"Are my eyes gold, too?"

"Yes they are, baby. You are magnificent. I have never seen a sexier wolf."

"What do I do now?"

"What do you want to do?" Malcolm nudged her neck with his snout.

"Run!"

"Then run, darlin'." Brax prodded her rump. *"We're right behind you."*

She needed no further urging. Rochelle leapt away and took off running. There were so many scents to sort out. She could smell the other pack members and identify each of them by smell alone. Her hearing picked up every little rustle, and she could see so clearly. It was as if it was daylight. A breeze swept along her coat, making her shiver, but it was a shudder of elation. Never had she felt so attuned to nature as she did at this moment.

Lifting her head, she howled at the moon, letting her song express her feelings. Her howl was echoed by every member of the pack, until lastly her mates joined in with her as she bayed again.

Her mates directed the path she took, and she went along with them since this was her first time out. They ended up in a clearing where a small lake shimmered in the light of the moon. Looking down as she padded to the edge of the water, she studied her reflection and chuffed before taking a drink. She thought she looked okay as a wolf, but since she hadn't been vain when in human form, she wasn't really concerned. All that mattered to her was that her mates seemed to like what she looked like in either form.

They ran and played for nearly two hours, but soon she wanted to head back to their rooms for a bath. The buildup to tonight had lasted a full week, and now she just wanted to be alone with her mates.

When they arrived at the edge of the garden once more, she watched as each of her mates changed back into their human form and dressed. Each of her men ran their fingers through her coat and scratched behind her ears. She moaned with delight and chuffed out a laugh. Now she knew why dogs liked to have their ears scratched.

"Look at me, darlin'." Brax gently held her face. "Concentrate on what you look like and how you feel when you are human and push your wolf back."

Rochelle did as Braxton suggested and felt her body begin to reshape. It seemed to her that it was a lot easier to change back to her original state than it had been to call forth her wolf. No doubt over time she would find it easier and easier to transform.

Jarrod passed her her clothes, and finally she was dressed. She intended to reach out and take Jarrod's and Brax's hands into hers, but Malcolm surprised her. Squealing in shock, she found herself swung off the ground and into his arms.

He grinned down at her and then began to walk toward the house. Instead of letting her down in the living room like she expected him to, Malcolm continued until they were outside the bedroom door.

"Close your eyes, Rochelle," he ordered quietly. "Good girl. Now keep them closed, and no peeking."

"What's going on?"

"You'll find out soon enough."

Malcolm moved again, and although she had the urge to peek, she didn't. The scent of flowers filled her nostrils, and Malcolm slid her down the length of his body until her feet were on the ground. He shifted again and pulled her down onto his lap.

"You can open your eyes now."

Rochelle gasped. The bed quilt was covered with the petals from roses and orchids. The floral scent permeated the room. Candles were lit and covered nearly every surface, and the light was turned down low.

"It's so beautiful. Thank you." She kissed Malcolm's lips and hugged him tight.

Malcolm smiled, stood up, and carried her toward the adjoining bathroom. After turning on and adjusting the faucets, he walked into the shower and took them both beneath the warm spray. Once they were both wet, he walked to the inset bench and sat with her on his lap once more.

Jarrod and Brax walked into the room, and she watched their naked bodies move from beneath her lowered lashes. Her libido, which had been simmering for the last couple of days, erupted into a raging inferno, and she wriggled on Malcolm's thighs.

"We'll take care of you, sweetness. Just relax and let us wash you." Malcolm's warm, moist breath tickled her ear and sent her horniness rocketing into the stratosphere.

Instead of doing what he said, she reached up and grabbed his hair and pulled his mouth down to hers. She kissed him with all the pent-up desire she was feeling and whimpered when he thrust his tongue into her mouth. She was burning up with sexual need and didn't want to wait anymore. So instead of stopping when she felt Jarrod and Braxton washing her, she just kept right on going. She didn't even stop when water flowed over her, rinsing her body.

Malcolm shifted and stood up straight, and she lifted her head to groan with frustration. More hands reached for her body, and she found herself wrapped in a towel and in Braxton's arms. She didn't want to wait for them to dry her. Rochelle wanted and needed her mates to love her now. And she wanted them all at the same time.

"Bed. Now!" she growled.

Chapter Fifteen

Brax dove for the bed and pulled her down with him. He ended up on his back with her on top of him. His big, muscular body was radiating heat, and that only made her burn hotter. Placing her hands on his cheeks, she lowered her head and slanted her mouth over his. *God sakes, my men all taste so good.*

She lifted slightly when hands pulled at the towel wrapping her body and sighed into Brax's mouth as their tongues danced. Rochelle had never felt so turned on. Just one touch from them could send her rocketing off into bliss.

More hands connected with her body and swept over her from shoulders to ass. She wiggled enticingly, seductively, begging Jarrod and Malcolm to touch her more intimately.

"Shh, baby, we know what you want. Let us take care of you and make you feel good," Jarrod rasped.

Fingers slipped down between her legs, and she mewled at the pleasurable contact to her aching flesh. She cried out when two fingers entered her pussy and stroked her dripping depths. The fingers were quickly removed, and then she was being lifted. She reached for Brax, and he took hold of her hips as her hands landed on his shoulders. Helping to align her body to his, he then began to press inside her wet pussy.

"Shit," Brax groaned. "You feel so good, darlin'. You are so fucking tight."

Rochelle felt the ache deep inside her alleviate slightly when Braxton's hard cock nudged against her womb. When she tried to rock her hips and move on him, he wrapped an arm around her waist and pulled her down onto his chest.

"Stay still, darlin', we don't want to hurt you."

"Move!" Rochelle demanded. "I need more, damn it."

"I'll give you more, baby," Jarrod said from close behind. "Just stay still."

Cold, wet fingers touched her anus, and she couldn't prevent her muscles from tightening. Jarrod didn't stop touching her, and he continued to talk to her until his fingers were all the way inside her ass. The sensation of having delicate, virgin nerves stroked was out of this world.

Her body was so primed she hoped she didn't explode before she had all her men's cocks in her body.

"Tell me if I hurt you, baby."

Speech was beyond her, so she grunted instead and concentrated on trying to keep her body relaxed as Jarrod began to press his erection into her bottom. The feeling took her breath away. She panted and pushed back against him, trying to alleviate the pinching burn to her back entrance. He didn't force his way in but took his time and gave her body time to adjust to the intrusion.

"I'm in, baby," Jarrod panted. "You've taken every single inch of me."

Using her arms, she pushed up from Braxton's chest and whimpered when the two cocks inside her body jerked and slipped a little deeper, but she was missing one of her men, and she needed to be connected to all of them. Turning her head, she sighed when she saw Malcolm waiting patiently beside her on his knees. The sexy bastard was stroking his own cock while looking at where her ass and cunt took his brothers.

"Malcolm."

He knew what she wanted and shifted closer. His hard dick brushed against her lips. She opened wide and sucked him in without preamble. There was no time to lick and tease. Rochelle wanted her men to come in her body as she climaxed with them. She began to bob her head up and down Malcolm's shaft, making sure to swirl her tongue around the sensitive crown of his cock when she retreated.

Giving a wiggle of her hips, she then moaned around the cock in her mouth when Jarrod and Braxton began to move inside her. They started off slow and in counterthrusts.

One advanced while the other retreated, but as they increased the speed of their sliding cocks, they changed the rhythm and angle of each thrust until finally her mates were fucking her at the same time. She wrapped her hand around the base of Malcolm's cock and pumped the flesh she couldn't take into her mouth. He was way too long, and she wasn't game to try and take him down her throat.

The groaning noises he made let her know that he was enjoying her ministrations. Rochelle's body felt like it was a rubber band being stretched taut with each stroke of her mates' cocks, and the tingling warmth which had been simmering began to flare out from her womb, down into her pussy and legs. She sobbed around Malcolm's cock, and he groaned.

"I'm gonna come, sweetness. It's up to you if you want to pull off or swallow."

Rochelle sucked him as deep as she could stand and groaned as his cock expanded and pulsed in her mouth. Warm jets of salty-sweet cum shot over her tongue and down her throat. She licked and sucked until he could take no more, and she released him with a pop as he collapsed on the bed beside them.

As she let go, the rubber band snapped. Rochelle screamed with rapturous pleasure as wave upon wave of bliss swept over her convulsing body. Her muscles clamped and released on the two cocks stroking in and out of her ass and pussy, but they didn't stop. They just kept right on going, making sure she rode out the waves of pleasure until the very end. Jarrod let out a deep, rumbling groan as his cock expanded in her ass and he shot her full of his cum.

Braxton followed scant seconds later, but he didn't groan—he roared as he filled her pussy full of semen. Still gasping for breath, the occasional aftershock wracking her body, she collapsed down on top of Brax. Her eyelids were heavy, and even though she was close to dozing she was still very much aware of what was going on around her.

Jarrod gently extricated his cock from her ass and got off the bed. Brax rolled them both over onto their sides, his semiflaccid cock slipping free from her body. Water ran in the bathroom, and then she was being cleaned up with a warm, soapy cloth, the scent of her familiar bodywash drifting to her nose. A dry towel followed, and then the mattress bounced and dipped as her men got comfortable.

"Will you marry us, darlin'?" Brax whispered into her ear as he cuddled her close.

Rochelle reached out for Malcolm. He was lying at the bottom of the bed, his hand resting on her thigh, and Jarrod was cuddled up to her back.

"Do you know how glad I am that I had to be changed into a werewolf?"

"We're happy if you are, sweetness." Rochelle nearly smiled when she heard the wariness in Jarrod's voice but held it back.

"Did you hear what Brax asked you, baby?"

"Do you know why I am glad I am now a werewolf?

"Why, darlin'?" Brax asked, but she could hear the frustration in his voice.

"Because now I know how good it feels to run on four paws and not stumble over my own feet. The wind ruffling through my fur feels like I'm being lightly petted, and I can now join you all each time you go out for a run. And lastly"—she gave them a sassy smile—"my eyes turn golden when I speak to you telepathically."

"We'll we're happy if you're happy, baby." Jarrod's voice sounded rather vexed.

Deciding she had teased them long enough, she said, "God sakes, I think we'd better get married real quick. I am so hungry I could eat a whole veggie garden, and the baby has only just been conceived. Just think about…"

Rochelle didn't get to finish her sentence because her three men started howling with joy, and then she was being smothered in love.

THE END

WWW.BECCAVAN-EROTICROMANCE.COM

ABOUT THE AUTHOR

My name is Becca Van. I live in Australia with my wonderful hubby of many years, as well as my two children.

I read my first romance, which I found in the school library, at the age of thirteen and haven't stopped reading them since. It is so wonderful to know that love is still alive and strong when there seems to be so much conflict in the world.

I dreamed of writing my own book one day but, unfortunately, didn't follow my dream for many years. But once I started I knew writing was what I wanted to continue doing.

I love to escape from the world and curl up with a good romance, to see how the characters unfold and conflict is dealt with. I have read many books and love all facets of the romance genre, from historical to erotic romance. I am a sucker for a happy ending.

For all titles by Becca Van, please visit
www.bookstrand.com/becca-van

Siren Publishing, Inc.
www.SirenPublishing.com

CPSIA information can be obtained at www.ICGtesting.com
Printed in the USA
BVOW03s1429021213

337918BV00019B/1326/P